Debt Collectors in Love

A NOVEL BY JOHN SANDMAN

Debt Collectors in Love

Whole Bean Books

Brooklyn, New York

Chapter One

I was almost asleep when I rolled the wrong way and saw the clock. 2:42 AM. If it's after four, you can say you're getting up early. If it's after three, it depends on how close it is to four. But 2:42 is in the middle of nowhere. I imagined sleep was something you could touch. When I reached across the bed it wasn't there.

The guy who'd been staying at my place for almost two months was gone. I met him at a conference I usually don't go to. He was the man who came for dinner and never left—a Brit, late 40s, about my age, who dumped London for New York.

He was very nice, almost too polite. I'd lie in the dark and hear that accent, which he called Hong Kong English because that's where he grew up. I loved his accent but didn't want him to feel self-conscious. I wanted to keep this light.

Right after this became an affair, five minutes after we had our clothes off, he said his wife left—would I marry him? I said no. Then he stayed and stayed. At first, when he left in the morning he'd say, "Do you want me to come back?" I always said yes. That became, "I'll see you tonight." He was interesting to talk to and brought me groceries. We'd cook, then sit on the couch and read before we went to bed. Sometimes we skipped reading. I went to the gym less.

He had a public relations job with the conference promoter. There was a phone on his desk that he never answered and he was never at his hotel. I wasn't sure where he was all day. I didn't really care. I needed a fling. I needed a distraction.

Neither of us had a mobile device. We're in the underground of people who don't have cell phones. I never gave him keys to my apartment because I believed this would end and when it did, I didn't want to ask for my keys back. So I still had to wait for the intercom and buzz him in. If he was the one to stop coming, I had less say than I thought about how it ended.

He *did* talk about leaving as much as he talked about staying. I never encouraged him to stay. And he left. One night when I went to bed there was no Geoff. Same thing the night after that and the night after that. I haven't counted the days, but it's been weeks. No one answered his work phone. E-mails didn't bounce. His clothes were gone, his tooth brush was still here. I wondered how he got his stuff out. It must have been the day I left for work early. My apartment door locks without keys.

The numbers on the clock kept turning. Eventually 2:42 was a long time ago. I've wasted hours trying to *think* I'd go to sleep. There must be research on this. I think of men in laboratories wearing white coats and chasing white mice. The search for an insomnia cure must keep them up all night.

Maybe Geoff got fired. I didn't think the internet would swallow the conference business, but they were already expensive when webinars appeared. Instead of flying to another city, staying in a hotel and having lunch served by uniformed waiters in a ballroom, you ate pizza watching a webinar on your computer. I had no idea whether webinars would multiply like rabbits.

Even if the marriage proposal was a ruse, his job wasn't. If he lost it I think he'd disappear. He told me, "I can't believe I'm here with you, I can't believe my good luck." If his luck ran out and he got canned, he'd probably rather go back to London than tell me. It could end just like that.

In a weird way I was still waiting for him so it was time to get up, no matter what the clock said. It was Saturday, but I was going to Lower Manhattan where I was a reporter at a financial newspaper. I found a bra and a hairbrush and was getting dressed in the dark, like I'd wake him if I turned on the lights.

I turned on a light. I couldn't take another step and fell into bed. When I woke up it was 12:53 in the afternoon. That got me going. I grabbed a sandwich. I almost forgot my keys.

The hallway outside had a long fluorescent light along the ceiling with black and white floor tiles. I lived across from a vacant apartment. Most mornings, Manny, the super, was there working. Most nights, too. The door opened slowly, then he popped out. He had dark eyebrows and a black beard. The gaps between his teeth were like the tiles on the floor.

"Hello, *mami!*"

"Hello."

"Early bird gets the worm?"

"It's one o'clock, Manny."

"What I'm sayin."

I started to stammer. "Have you seen my friend Geoff?"

"That dude that been comin around? Naw, I ain't seen him. Is he movin out?"

"What do you mean?"

"Cause his name's not on the lease, Miss Pigeon. He can't be livin here."

"What makes you think he lived here?"

"I see him in the building a lot. But not lately."

I was fuming. *Forget it, Kay,* I thought. After forgot it, I said, "Suppose he was my friend who liked to visit a lot?"

"Be smart. I'd have to snitch if you keep on."

"Beg pardon?"

"It's on the lease up in here. No unrelated people in the same unit. If I rat you out to management, I'm just doin my job."

"Is ratting me out part of your job description?"

"Don't got a job description. Just a job."

"What about Grace across the hall?"

"Who?"

"Grace Fong. She has two roommates living with her. Even though they have the same last name, they're not related."

"Oh, no, they definitely related." Manny smiled. "They all sisters to me."

Manny picked up his paint can as I left. I could feel his eyes on me all the way down the hall. I thought what he said about my lease wasn't true—and that Manny might be able to force me out of here while I could do nothing about the drug trade on the ground floor where he was a player. It was mainly a drive-by market that came over the George Washington Bridge. Investment bankers from Jersey, hedge fund managers from Connecticut, perhaps? If that's who it was, Manny worked on Wall Street, too.

I was so glad to get an apartment that I didn't read my lease. The place was big enough for my kids to live there as teenagers. We came here from Missouri about ten years ago. The idea that Geoff couldn't move in because we weren't related was making me irate. And I didn't even want him to move in.

The elevator had that New York elevator smell. It gets off with you in the lobby, which still has a whiff of the way it looked in better days. It was also real slow. I was about to take the stairs when I heard the whirring noise come up from the lobby. The elevator stopped as the apartment door across the hall opened. Wensi Fong, Grace Fong's roommate, walked out.

Her hair was in a bouffant that made her seem a foot taller. The fragrance she wore came off like hair spray. She got on and stood across from me.

"You're looking fabulous," I said.

Wensi looked at the floor. "Why thank you, Kay."

"Is this for work or fun?"

"I don't mix business with pleasure."

"That's smart. So, business or pleasure?"

She didn't answer. I wondered if she'd heard me talking to Manny. I should have left it there.

"How's your student loan?" I asked.

Her voice had an edge. "How's yours?"

"It sucks. Really, Wensi, I'm just chatting you up."

She didn't reply. When we got off, she went toward the basement entrance, I went out the front door. I was still groggy. I forgot to make coffee.

I walked to the subway at 181st Street, three stops from the end of the A train in Upper Manhattan. I live on Fort Washington Avenue, about two blocks west of Broadway. Depending on who you ask, this was Washington Heights, Hudson Heights or the Dominican Heights. The station is deep underground. It was October 2011. The train would be crowded and make all the local stops because it was Saturday.

Seeing Wensi reminded me that I was going to work on a story about student loan servicers. That's not part of my job, but this newspaper's days were numbered and I'd been thinking about alternatives. That could mean two freelance jobs and waiting until one—or both—ended. I was expecting a call from Europe at the office.

What are student loan servicers? They're the people that call to demand your loan payments. They aren't thugs pounding on your door, they're customer service reps at a call center, sitting behind a computer, wearing a headset with a mouth piece, reading the answers to your questions from a script.

My daughter, Eileen—we call her Leenie—got Stafford Loans from the federal Department of Education to go to graduate school. We thought she'd graduate, get a good job and pay them off quickly. Instead, she got a low-paying job in the food service industry—she was lucky to have that—and struggled with the payments. The student loans are the elephant in the room—hers and mine, since we live in separate places. I can imagine Leenie in an assisted living facility in 2061, her false teeth clacking in her head when somebody says, "Remember those old student loans from around the turn of the century, Leenie dear?" "Remember?" says Leenie, "I'm still paying mine off!" Nobody laughs.

There's a limit on what you could borrow from Stafford and she needed federal Grad PLUS Loans to make up the difference. As an undergrad at Hunter College she had a business refurbishing old athletic shoes and selling them to classmates. She'd get Nikes or Converse Chuck Taylor All-Stars and work on them in her room, reinforcing the soles, putting in new linings and laces and spray painting them gold or black. She'd refurbish 10 pairs of Chucks at a time. Her shoe makeovers were cool and made some money—it actually seemed promising. What if she had gone into footwear instead of film school? Was that the happy ending she flubbed?

But she got a credit card from a salesman she

met at Hunter and used it for shoe materials, then had a dispute with a supplier. She couldn't get her money back and stopped paying the card. By the time she needed the Grad PLUS Loans, she was delinquent on $2200. To get the PLUS Loans she needed a co-signer. That had to be me.

I've had car loans but always paid on time. I've had *one* credit card, no late payments—ever. But I didn't read Leenie's loan documents like I didn't read my apartment lease. I think there are millions of people who hear the words *student loan* and think *free money.* Leenie was one of them. So was I.

I wasn't thinking about this when Leenie sat at my kitchen table plotting her move to California. She convinced me that she had to get a master's degree in film. She did really well at Hunter College which cost practically nothing compared to what you'd pay to be on some leafy New England campus. Both of us were feeling smart. There was also her math geek older brother, Rod. He did a four-year degree at Baruch College with no debt and got an MBA through his job in finance. I wanted her to follow in some of his footsteps but live her own life and make her own mistakes. I didn't think getting student loans would be a mistake— it's money to go to college, not to a casino. I never thought of this as a gamble.

At first, she wanted to work in television as a set designer then thought why think small and applied to the production and director tracks at film schools in LA. The school she picked was hard to get into—I can't say the name of that place anymore. I didn't think about money. Because this is *good debt,* I didn't worry about the interest rates.

When the A train came I got a seat next to a man-spreading dude who couldn't keep his legs closed. He was taking up room for two people. I don't concede anything to these guys. They push on me, I push back. It was a few more stops before I had enough room to get out my calculator. I was still crunching numbers on these loans, thinking that if I find a mistake we'll owe less money and this will be less bad. Only I never find it.

Stafford charged around 7% interest, the Grad PLUS about 8% plus a 4% loan origination fee. She got grants from the school, but Stafford Loans max out at around $20,000 per year. She needed more and the rest came from the PLUS Loans. Altogether, she owed $142,147— her debt at graduation. That's 30 grand more than my annual salary.

The interest on PLUS begins to accrue when you get your money. You can borrow huge amounts for grad school, up to the total cost of attendance—rent, food, six margaritas during Happy Hour, it all adds up. The schools know this—they keep raising tuition and will always get paid. One night I woke up and thought, *I'm not just subsidizing my daughter with this debt, I'm subsidizing this school.*

The first year was ok, but her last year she made a movie. What I thought about it wasn't important, it was what other people thought and nobody liked it. It took me a while to admit I didn't like it, either. That was shocking. When I cut to the chase, film school was looking like a mistake.

Her advisors said don't worry—film school is a place where it's ok to fail. It wasn't. To pay for the privilege of failing, she had to borrow all this money. She graduated into a bad job market and stayed in California to be near the industry. She lives in LA, where she wanted to be, but works in a restaurant, a million miles from where she wanted to be. I wanted her to move back to New York because of the loans—she could live rent free with me for a while. She said no. Eventually I stopped sending her money. She wouldn't tell me how she made up for the money I stopped sending her.

She refused to consolidate her Stafford and Grad PLUS Loans, where they'd become one loan with one cheaper monthly payment. I was furious. One of her LA friends, Rihanna, who got private student loans, convinced her that loan consolidation was a scam. Leenie moved in with Rihanna and two guys near the Pomona Freeway in El Monte—they all have student loans. Leenie holds my age against me but she's 24 and living with people about my age. When we're on the phone I'm like, "Who are these people?" She goes, "People with student loans. We've come out about our student loans and we're in solidarity." I saw Rihanna ranting on YouTube about her private student loans from Sallie Mae. She now owes three times more than when she left school. Their message to Leenie is: you'll have student loans the rest of your life, get over it.

What if this becomes like a student loan cult group? I've assumed she wouldn't become like her roommates—stuck with student loans when they're retired and having their Social Security benefits grabbed by the government to pay them off. But Leenie's life is ahead of her and who knows what that will be like. I just know that she has this debt.

Then she started having sex with these people. I can hear her now. "People who have student loans together might as well have sex together. That's better than no sex—and we can't afford to go on a date." They probably can't afford condoms. If I question her, she goes, "Oh, c'mon *Mom!* They're not that different from the people *you* have sex with, so don't be so irate."

I'm afraid she'll do her own Facebook or YouTube posts. Then she finally gets a job interview, but they find her student loan social media rants and stop calling. If I'm wondering what happens next, I'm wondering alone. Leenie and I are estranged. That's what I hate most about this. It all started with these goddam loans. We had our problems before, but this is different.

Payments on PLUS came due when she got the last installment—a semester before she graduated. There was no grace period. You can get a six-month deferment after graduation, but the interest still accrues. When the deferment ends, the balance is higher than when you started. By the fall of 2010 she was out of school but not making enough to pay for the Stafford *and* the PLUS Loans. I had a payment coupon booklet from the loan servicer, just no checks from Leenie.

I suggested she re-start her shoe business. Her answer was *Like, NO, that would be admitting I'm a TOTAL FAILURE!* I was at a loss. I set up an auto-debit with my bank where the servicer would withdraw a payment for the PLUS Loans every month and forgot about it.

Six months later, the loan servicer called. That's how I met Doris Morris.

It started at 8:00 AM. The person on the line said, "It's Doris from Pennsylvania Higher Ed."

"And you're calling about what?"

"Eileen Snopes. You know her?"

"She's my daughter."

"Right, we're the servicer of your Grad PLUS Loans. You just went 90 days delinquent on your payments. You co-signed Eileen's loans so you're on the hook."

I dropped the phone and asked her to repeat that. She ignored me and began reading from a script that described this Dante's *Inferno* for people who get crushed by these federal loans. It starts with delinquency, when you miss one payment, and can end with default, where the penalties and interest explode.

Credit bureaus are notified after a late payment. Your credit score starts to crash. Car dealers, landlords and banks all find out. If you go into default, there can be a garnishment, where your employer sends part of your paycheck to the lender before you see it. You also lose your income tax refund. Win the lottery? They take that, too. Default, said Doris, is the jackpot you don't want to hit.

I'd made payments for three months to a loan servicer in Missouri. Then the loan was switched to a servicer in Pennsylvania. Doris wouldn't explain how this Pennsylvania servicer, called FedLoan, took over and why I wasn't notified. When I asked why my payments weren't going through, Doris became irate and hung up.

My bank couldn't tell me why the auto-debit payments stopped. The servicer in Missouri had no answers. When I tried to set up a new auto-debit payment, it didn't work. I thought, *ok, I'll send a check.*

The day the check cleared FedLoan phoned three times to say I was delinquent. "You're going into default," Doris screamed. "You're gonna blow your credit score! Then you can't borrow!" They didn't always know how many payments I missed. They were vague about how much I owed. The monthly payment was about $480 when I started. It went higher.

I told Doris I didn't like the way my account was being managed and wanted to change servicers. She laughed and hung up. I didn't know what to do. None of this made sense. Who decided that this company in Pennsylvania got to be the loan servicer? If I didn't like my bank I can find another. Why can't I change my student loan servicer?

I sent them money every month since Doris started calling but the calls didn't stop—there were several messages a day, even after checks cleared. When I went to my online account, I found that the PLUS wasn't getting paid because the payment I sent was applied to the Stafford—not PLUS. Fedloan serviced both loans. I called and called. I couldn't get this fixed.

Other Fedloan people called. One called me a bitch when I yelled at her. Because I didn't want them to think they were getting to me, I didn't complain. But they were getting to me. I didn't know who these people were. They were voices in the night—and it was often dark when they called.

In June other people besides Doris called. I was six months behind on the PLUS while my payments went to the Stafford. Leenie must have noticed because she wasn't paying every month, but that loan was current because of my payments.

There was a week when nobody called, then Doris was back. Her voice was sometimes high-pitched, other times she would warble. Sometimes she sounded intelligent. She often sounded stupid and made dumb grammatical mistakes. But her laugh was deep and loud. She was a different person when she laughed— she laughed *at* you, like she was enjoying your misery.

By August Geoff was around. I was glad—I

thought less about the loans and stopped answering the phone. When it kept ringing he'd say, "Why don't you answer your phone?" "Old boyfriend," I replied. That made him more curious, not less. Then he'd ask what I did in bed with this imaginary person who was really Doris.

I didn't stop answering the phone for long. I'm like Pavlov's dog. When it rings, I answer. Something weird happened when the loans went from the Missouri servicer to Fedloan. A year ago, I had no debt. Maybe I needed a lawyer.

I finally called one who said Fedloan wasn't allowed to phone before 8 AM or after 9 at night. They called much earlier and as late as midnight. I wrote Fedloan a letter demanding that the calls stop. They admitted that some of those calls were illegal. Then they removed my phone number from my account page and locked me out so I couldn't make website payments or get loan documents. To regain access to my account, I had to type in my phone number and click a box saying I agreed to have them phone me. They started calling again. They wouldn't say their first and last names. They never identified themselves by both their first *and* last name. It was either, "Hi, it's Jane from Fedloan" or, "Hi, it's Mrs. Jane from Fedloan"—never both names.

Doris Morris was different because she usually couldn't separate her first and her last name. It almost never came out Doris or Ms. Morris, but as one word: DorisMorris. Sometimes she'd identify herself as Ms. Morris, but I still knew it was her. Her voice was distinctive.

By September—last month—I made a website payment that again went to the Stafford instead of the PLUS and I fell another month behind. This is when I started to lose it. One morning somebody from Fedloan

I didn't know called and I'm screaming "Give me Doris Morris!" The Fedloan woman asked why and I yelled: "Because I said so—bitch!"

I was on hold, then bounced around for 20 minutes. I was late for work, but I thought this was my chance to give *somebody* a piece of my mind. If I got flunked back to "Get me your supervisor" I didn't care.

Doris came on the phone. Before I could open my mouth, she started apologizing in one long run-on sentence for the way I'd been treated and for things she hadn't done. I couldn't get a word in edgewise. She had to hang up but she'd call back about *my issue.*

The next morning, she called and read from her script.

"This is Doris from Fedloan, calling with reference to your Grad PLUS Loans. This is an attempt to collect a debt."

There was a silence.

"Doris? You there?"

"I'm here."

"Is this an attempt to collect a debt? I thought you we were finding out about *my issue.*"

"This is an attempt to tip you off about how you're getting screwed by Fedloan."

I just got out of the shower. I had nothing to write on. Everything was wet. "How do I get screwed?"

"You know what Fedloan really is don't you?"

"I *think* I know who *they* are but I'm not sure what *you* are."

"We're hired by the federal government to service student loans. Fedloan says they're a loan servicer. I think they're really a debt collector. That's how they make their money and they couldn't care less about whaddiacall, *students.* They're not as bad as your collection agencies but close."

"What kind of debts?"

"Just student loans. Sometimes we're there to crush the borrower. Sometimes we break the law to get you to pay. Then there's the crazy shit going on inside this call center. What happens by accident is as bad as what gets done on purpose when the CSRs don't know what they're doing."

"What's a CSR?"

"A customer service rep. There's different names for it." She laughed. "I been called a lotta names."

The years I worked in newspapers left me with a sense of knowing when people wanted to talk, when they didn't and when coaxing them to say something was worthwhile. I also have a sense for when people are lying, when they're exaggerating, when they're telling the truth and when they're confused about what the truth really is. If she's sitting there with my life story as a Grad PLUS Loan co-signer on her computer screen, she knows I work for a newspaper.

Suddenly, she couldn't talk. I said call me back.

A week later she phoned but not from her work number. I didn't know it was her until she said, "Hi, it's Doris Morris."

"Hi," I said. I was on my way out the door. "So where were we? Didn't you say you had something for me about the loans?"

"You write for a newspaper, right?"

"The news we write is kind of obscure."

"Well, I got news for you."

"It might not be news we can use."

"I'm ready to dish about loan servicing and debt collection and how borrowers with student loans get screwed and get defrauded."

"Which borrowers?"

"Any borrower. Like for instance, they'll tell us to

push people that can't pay into forbearance even when there's better deals. Forbearance is when you can temporarily stop making payments on your loans, but the interest keeps accruing. We could tell you about income driven repayment plans—that's better for you— but they take too long to set up with all the paperwork. Forbearance is quick, we do it over the phone. We put a note in your file, print out a letter—boom!"

"Boom?"

"So by the time you're out of forbearance, you owe more than when you started. That's more money for the federal government and the loan servicer and more debt for you. And that ain't the half of it. Do you want to, like, talk?"

"In general, yeah. I cover big banks, but not consumer loans. That doesn't mean I won't later, but I don't want to mislead you about what I can do with this right now."

"It's not a problem."

"And I'd like to meet you in person."

"Not a problem."

"You're in Pennsylvania," I said. "I'm here."

"No problem. I'm coming to you. I quit the call center and I'm moving to New York. We'll be in the same place. I saw that website of your newspaper with your picture. Really, I want to tell my story."

I was going to ask why she quit but was too busy thinking about how much I resented her. It wasn't enough that she was dangling some crazy reversal of fortune.

"Ok," I said. "Call me when you get here." We exchanged e-mail addresses. She hung up.

Then I forgot about it. The phone calls from Fedloan kept on coming, just not from Doris. My last payment went to the Stafford again—not the PLUS loan, driving it deeper into the red. No one could explain why I got switched from the first servicer to Fedloan or why my payments weren't being applied to the PLUS Loans. I couldn't give this my undivided attention. There were problems at work.

At times I was in despair. Leenie insisted Fedloan hadn't called her but I had a hard time believing that after I heard from my 85-year-old aunt in Montana who said they were calling *her.* I couldn't believe my poor aunt, who I hadn't seen in 30 years, was being harassed over money I didn't actually borrow.

Doris e-mailed a photo of herself in a parking lot with red lipstick applied to her big mouth and curly blond hair popping out of her head. She reminded me of an old-time movie star—Clara Bow, Mary Pickford, somebody from silent films. She was wearing pink tights and a green T-shirt that said *I'm From the Keystone State* with the Pennsylvania state symbol. It wasn't the sinister image I had of her. She didn't say why she came here but found a place in Queens and was working in a word processing pool at a law firm. She went from one kind of digital sweatshop to another. Queens was a long subway ride from Washington Heights.

But her office was blocks away from mine in Lower Manhattan. She sent me e-mails saying we should meet. I didn't think she was serious. But I found myself researching the student loan servicers. There was obviously a story here, one that Doris could help me with. What I didn't like was that it was my story. And Leenie's.

Chapter Two

The A train crawled into 42nd Street and went out of service. I took the local the rest of the way. I should have brought something to read from my student loan clip file instead of crunching Leenie's numbers. I thought about what I told Doris, that I wrote about big banks, not consumer loans and that they were far apart. It wasn't that simple.

About 90% of student loans are from the federal government. If the U.S. Department of Education was a bank, it'd be one of the world's biggest. These are consumer loans and banks are lenders also. Some banks originated federal student loans that were guaranteed by the government when the borrower defaulted.

After the 2008 financial crisis, millions of people couldn't pay their mortgages, but lenders had their houses as collateral. With a mortgage, the bank can take your home. With an auto loan, they can take your auto. With a student loan, nobody's going to repossess your art history degree.

You could often keep your house or car in a bankruptcy but it's almost impossible to write off a federal student loan if you go bankrupt unless you can prove undue hardship---that's a heavy lift. Federal student loans could be included in a bankruptcy until the mid-1970s, when Congress started to change the laws. It's like the government is preventing you from filing a true bankruptcy if you have one of their loans— as if bankruptcy will make your life sublime. It doesn't matter if a court says you're broke. If you have one of these loans, they're coming after the money you need to live on.

In 2010 the government stopped guaranteeing new federal student loans made by banks. A lot of banks left the market after that. But there were already billions of dollars in loans made before 2010 still in repayment. Banks are still covered by the federal government when the borrower defaults. Borrowers have no such luck. Their phones keep ringing.

Thousands of trolls like Doris are foot soldiers in the war against people who can't afford the rising cost of higher ed. Whether they worked for the loan servicer or a collection agency, they were there for one reason—to collect. I didn't have the big picture yet. I knew what was happening to me but I didn't know what I didn't know.

Then here comes Doris Morris who wants to dish about debt collection. The story could include someone who went after borrowers. Could anyone trust what Doris had to say? The answer might be a long time in coming.

Borrowers with student loan stories were all over the internet. What you couldn't find was somebody who'd tell the lender side without asking to be paid. Doris hadn't mentioned money. She could string me along, then tell me about her fees. Money could be why she wanted to meet. Money was why I was talking to her in the first place. This all started because my daughter got student loans so she could start her working life. What could be more benign?

Meanwhile, I have this full-time newspaper job, but that newspaper could disappear. I thought it was disappearing now. Strange people had been appearing in the halls. Word got around that a hedge fund from Bahrain that moved into private equity wanted to buy us. One day I found some guy standing near my desk staring at me. Just staring. I didn't know who he was but I could feel what was happening. He didn't need a name tag that said HELLO I'm _____.

Geoff came after the student loan story idea arrived. I didn't want to dump this on him because I wasn't sure what he'd say. I did it anyway. He said if you can do it without quitting your day job—do it. I didn't tell him that I might have to do this *instead* of my day job.

The hope was that I could turn this into a story that helped me get into the consumer finance beat somewhere, a long, long shot. Around when Geoff was pushing his let's-get-married thing, I started bringing papers to bed about the history of student loans and how they're regulated. It started with pages from the *Federal Register*. Then the federal Department of Education website. Then FinAid.org, FastWeb, Student Loan Justice, the National Consumer Law Center, the Woodstock Institute and other dot orgs. Newspapers smudged the pillows with ink.

I'm a shade under six feet tall, Geoff was six-foot-three, so we already take up a lot of space. He would reach for me and get a face full of paper, then roll to the edge of the bed to get out of the way.

Around then I met a woman at an art gallery who was looking for stories like this one for a new news website. One that would pay. She kept saying, "Oh, and we pay!" We left and talked for a while afterward and she sounded hot for this story. It seemed that there might be a place I could go if this newspaper folded, a door that I could get my foot in. The number of people who defaulted on their student loans was stunning. There were millions of them. They owed billions.

It became an opportunity to coax Geoff toward

the door. I was probably nudging him to go more than I thought. Part of me wanted him to stay, part of me wanted him to go. This was pushing me toward the side that said *go*. It helped me send the following message: no, you can't hang out indefinitely so I can marry you and you can get your green card and stay here legally, assuming that's where this was leading and I don't know how that works. If it became a sham marriage and we walked away from it later, if everybody was sort of ok with that, I still didn't like it. I'd been married twice before. That became a sham, too, even if it was different.

Geoff would profess his love. He would swear that he and his wife were through, which won't clinch your deal like it could once upon a time. But he may have seen the end coming even if I didn't, even if I'd already been thinking about it. If it came slowly or all at once, I wouldn't know. That probably mattered more than I think so I won't think about it.

He was the kind to leave a note on my door. The risk was I'd catch him in the act and who knows where that would lead. But there was no note. I could feel his presence—feel it receding.

My bed was going to fill up with paper. I could stop worrying about insomnia if I was up late reading about the student loan crisis. After he was gone, the paper was going to grow wild like ivy on the side of a building. My sense of smell is acute. I'd notice when his scent finally faded. Washing the sheets a few times would do the trick.

Chapter Three

The building was near the tip of Manhattan where I took the elevator to the 22nd floor. The newspaper was called *Securities International News,* also known as *SIN*. It belonged to a reclusive Canadian newspaper magnate's publishing empire before being spun off into another company with 20 other publications. Most were heavy on newsprint, light on the web.

You'd forget the company's name as soon as you heard it. It's like a thorny rosebush with dying niche publications on its branches instead of roses. This was the financial trade press, where publications cover verticals like banking, insurance, commercial real estate—the list is long. Some were held together by staples, some weren't, and some were printed on this tacky paper like the kind you'd wrap birthday presents with. When most of them began to flounder, the company that was created in the spin-off went on the block. Nobody wanted it until the hedge fund from Bahrain started coming around.

Like the marketing campaign says, *SIN* covers operations, technology and compliance in the securities industry. The term *securities* refers mainly to stocks and bonds and is misleading. Securities can be real insecure. They can lose value and you can lose your money. But we don't write just for traders. We write for government regulators, computer geeks, market structure and market data freaks, from the front end where brokers execute trades to the back office where people settle trades and shuffle paper. There's less paper as everything goes digital.

The term "SIN" was in the paper's clunky web address but the extension is .net, not .com. If you type in sin.com, there's a screen full of bare asses instead of stories about data aggregators. Some people became very somber. Others laughed. It wasn't my problem.

Editorial was on 22, I took the stairs to the 23rd floor where the finance people were. The place looked deserted until I went by the conference room. There was a stack of pizza boxes outside the door. Through the blinds I could see strange people, probably from the hedge fund, sitting around a table with people from management. Even though I'd worked here for ten years, I suddenly felt like I was somewhere I didn't belong. I went down to 22.

At the bottom of the stairs I saw my editor, Lenny Shrank, head for the elevator. I owed him a story that I didn't file on Friday—another reason I came in today. Standing there talking to me would be proof that he didn't rate a seat at the table where the hedge fund deal was going down—and probably never would. It would also be evidence that we were working on the weekend again. Who wanted to talk about that?

I heard the elevator. He was gone. I should have said something. I owed him other things besides that story. Sometimes I forget.

I went to my desk which was near his. There was no one around but another reporter, Kara Markakis. She ignored me, I ignored her. Kara won a Neal award in 2003, the trade press equivalent of an Oscar—they're incredibly hard to get. She became insufferable after that. It was mounted on the wall over her desk.

I turned on my computer and went to a student loan website while I waited for the phone to ring.

The first call would probably be from Brussels, headquarters of Euroclear, and I'd be hearing from one Mathias Fokker. Euroclear cleared and settled trades in Europe. Like many people in Scandinavia and the Benelux countries, Mathias Fokker spoke fluent English. It was his accent that got in the way. I often couldn't understand him and his American PR guy would be interrupting and being difficult. I spoke to Mathias Fokker once a week. The only way to make this work was to tape the call and play it back until I figured out what he was saying. Taping him was a must.

I could have done this from my apartment but for the phone connection. One night the building was struck by lightning. I was alone. My bedroom lit up and turned white. I thought the end of the world was near. When it went dark again I thought the end was here. The darkness continued as my eyes adjusted. There was some rain against the window and lightning in New Jersey. Whatever happened was over.

Everything was fine except for the phone on my bedroom desk, a landline. It was blinking off and on like a wind-up toy. There was no dial tone. I bought a new phone but when I tried to hook up my tape recorder it didn't work. Another phone and a new tape recorder later and nothing happened. Manny the super wasn't interested in looking at this. Neither was my phone company. I found somebody who got fired by the phone company who offered telecom services. He said he'd come over. I crossed my fingers.

A week later he shows up with a phone company badge and a tool kit.

"Hello," I said. "I thought you weren't with the phone company anymore."

"I'm not," he replied. "Wearing this badge helps remind me of where I've been and who I am. Or at least where I've been."

All the wires were in the bedroom. He stopped in front of the bed and I pointed to my phone. "When I hook up my tape recorder it doesn't work. I can't tape calls."

He gave me a funny look. "What do you want to tape calls for?"

"My job."

"Who are you taping?"

"Geeks. Plain old geeks."

"What kind of geeks?"

"Tech geeks. Banking geeks." I yawned. "Really boring geeks."

"Do you know who Monica Lewinsky is?"

"Of course."

"Do you know who Linda Tripp is?"

I yawned.

"Did you know that's against the law?"

"This is for my job."

"What's your job?"

"No, this is fine. The people I'm recording *want* to be recorded. They're less likely to be misquoted than if I'm trying to write down what they say while I'm doing an interview."

"What are they saying?"

"Real esoteric stuff. Beyond obscure."

His eyes narrowed. "Have you ever been in jail?"

"What's that got to do with fixing my phone?"

"Because if you tape-record phone calls, you could go to jail."

"It's legal in New York."

"What if they changed the law? Would you even know?"

"Who'd know that I'm taping calls? What are you gonna do, drop a dime on me?"

"You know what I'm trying to do for you? I'm looking out for you and trying to keep you out of trouble."

"You know what you can do for me instead of look out for me? Fix my phone!"

The next thing I know I'm arguing with this fake phone company guy who won't fix my phone. After he'd been there an hour I figured out the problem. He *couldn't* fix my phone because he didn't know how. After he left somebody else came over—he couldn't fix it, either. There's probably some wireless workaround that won't work.

So I have to be at SIN to tape people. What would I do if the newspaper folded and I had to freelance from home and couldn't tape anyone. I began to think that what was wrong had nothing to do with the lightning strike. Either way I needed a tape recorder for my phone.

Another call might be Leenie. Sometimes we talked on Saturday afternoon—it's morning in LA—and I said I'd be at work. We can't be that estranged if we're still talking. But we had less and less to say. You'd think my famous interviewing skills could keep the conversation going. Now and then I'd bring up the topic of when she was a little girl, when Leenie, her older brother Rod, her father and I lived together, when we were fairly happy, when we were *normal* by some bygone definition. Even that looked bad. She called from a communal phone in her house, a land line.

Talking about her job search was out. I stopped asking about the roommates. Every few days I went to YouTube to see if she posted any videos of herself ranting about student loans. So far there was nothing. I felt funny about doing that at work. I couldn't be sure who was watching. Although a lot of the guys at this place watched porn or day traded at their desks.

I wrote out questions for Leenie, like she was a geek who would scorn my tech knowledge. I already had some for Mathias Fokker that were all tech and not personal. There was Euroclear and there was Clearstream. They competed in the European securities clearing business. We could start there, maybe fit in a question about how he thought European Economic and Monetary Union was doing, where countries in Western Europe replaced their national currencies with the euro. There was no more German mark, no more French franc, which once had portraits of French authors on the folding money. Even though that began in 1999, people still asked: could monetary union eventually fail without fiscal and political union? That usually made the European Union technocrats crazy. I didn't have a dog (or a cat) in that fight.

Geoff used to live in Brussels. He had an EU passport and talked about moving to Paris with me. I know some French but nixed that idea, too. Regardless of what language we spoke, I couldn't think seriously about moving to Paris, with or without him, because of this student debt overhang. I don't think he understood that. Where he comes from 50-year-old people don't have student loans.

I went back to the questions for Leenie and was completely stumped. I couldn't tell who would call first. Probably Mathias Fokker. Sometimes a guy from the Financial Services Authority in London checked in with me on the weekend. In the fall there was a conference in Amsterdam that I always go to, but this year there was no travel budget. That worried me. Trying to monitor this geek fest from New York was no substitute for being there in person. I'd be sitting here with a news hole on technical issues that I couldn't fill. Not sending me to that conference was another sign that this newspaper was in trouble.

I opened a story on multi-asset class trading that I owed Lenny. When that went nowhere, I fished out my calculator. I've got my own fetishes and re-running the numbers on the PLUS Loans was one of them. If I'm on the phone and get put on hold, I'll get out the calculator. If I'm stuck on a story and waiting to get unstuck, I'll get it out again.

Even if I found an error and got it fixed, they could still apply my payments to the wrong loan. That's where they continue to screw me over and I don't know how to stop it.

The phone rang, reminding me that I needed a new work phone, too. The window above the number pad that identified the caller blinked off last week. I couldn't see who it was before I answered. I picked up on the fourth ring.

"Hello Kay Pigeon."

"Hi, it's Doris."

"Excuse me?"

"Doris Morris."

"Oh—Doris...how'd you find me here?"

"From when I worked at Fedloan. I called you at home and when you didn't answer, I thought I'd try here."

"I didn't know you had my work number."

"We always had your work number. I never used it because I didn't want to get you in trouble at your job. Sometimes we'd call people about their student loans at work and they got fired."

I was expecting the measured, civilized tone of Mathias Fokker on the other side of the Atlantic or the monosyllabic Leenie, 20 minutes from the Pacific Ocean depending on traffic—not the piercing, warbly voice of

Doris Morris.

"Well, Doris...I had no idea."

"We said we'd talk, right?"

I was going to tell her I was expecting another call. But an e-mail came in from Leenie. She couldn't phone me. It wasn't a good time. She'd try next week. I started to write back, then stopped. I didn't know what to say. I typed *OK* but didn't send it.

"Kay? You there?"

"Yeah, I'll be here awhile longer."

"Let's talk tonight. I was gonna ask if you wanna meet at the gym."

"The gym?"

"The one across the street from your office. The New York Health Boutique. I just joined. I'm going from work and I brang extra workout clothes. They're probably a little small—or a little big—but maybe they'd kinda fit ya. We could meet up."

"I wasn't planning on that."

"Make new plans."

I lowered the phone. I sent the message to Leenie that said *OK*. Actually, I'd brought my own clothes. And that gym she joined, the New York Health Boutique, was my gym. It was a chain, not a boutique. I was going there after I left here. This was reminding me that I had to get to know this person again, who I didn't really know.

"Ok, Doris, I'll meet you out front at five."

"Just come inside. I'll give your name to the desk."

She hung up before I could say that I was a member, too. I thought of calling her back but didn't have her number. Or a caller ID screen that worked.

I wrote Leenie a paragraph. After I clicked *send* e-mail came from the editor of the new news website I met at that art gallery. *How's the student loan call center story going?* she wrote. *Fine*, I wrote back. *I'll be able to tell you more in a few days.* A message popped in from Mathias Fokker. He was being delayed; could we reschedule? *Great*, I wrote. *How about Monday?* A message came from his flack: *Monday works.* That would give me more time to figure out how to handle Doris Morris.

I was having second thoughts about the new news website. First, they haven't been around very long. Second, I didn't trust them.

But I was afraid to pitch the student loan story somewhere else, like a big news organization where I knew no one, then never hear from them while they tried to follow my lead. I'd been at this newspaper long enough so that I wasn't up to date on the industry. I'd already met the new news website's editor and I liked her, I liked bouncing ideas off her. But I had no idea what made them tick. If they were living on venture capital and the click count drops, their investors could step in and switch from news to porn or something else. If it's easier to start a website than a newspaper, it's probably easier to shut one down. I have no idea about any of this.

Upstairs they were probably handing this place over to the hedge fund. Then somebody else could get us, take us apart and sell the pieces. A few publications could survive and the rest would close. Everyone's days could be numbered. We might have a year left or it could be a matter of months. The next big event would be working out with Doris. Working out with people you don't know can be the worst kind of ice breaker.

I was a volleyball player in high school. Then the boys I hung around with said you shouldn't be playing volleyball, you should be with us so that stopped for a while. I played in college, then quit school. Why I started working out again wasn't to improve my health. I didn't look in the mirror and see stretch marks. I stood outside Leenie's bedroom and smelled dope. Her brother Rod had moved out. She liked having the room to herself, but we were both feeling bereft. Even if he ended up someplace worse he was still leaving us behind. I wondered if smoking dope didn't help her fill the void.

It was raining. I knocked on the door and said, "Hey Leenie, let's go for a run." "A run?" she said. "A run where?" I suggested a run in a park. Or in the street.

She agreed. That's how stoned she was. I wasn't a runner then, but I had running shoes and sweats, I don't know where they came from. Leenie had them from school. We went out into the pouring rain and ran for about a mile.

That was one of the few times we ran together. After that she stopped smoking dope in her room. There were other places she could go to get stoned if she had a mind and I don't know if she found them. It was the best I could do to get in the way of any drugs she was using which we talked about, calmly. She never became a regular drug user as far as I knew. I'm not pro or con legalizing cannabis, I just don't want her to get busted or have a car accident because she drove stoned.

After she moved out, I kept running. I joined a gym. By then I was doing two-hour workouts and it became one more thing we weren't going to do together.

It all started because I was concerned about Leenie and drugs. Working out became like a drug. I'd feel loopy if I stayed away from the gym for more than a few days. Sometimes I can do dozens of push-ups. Not those push-ups with your knees on floor, but real push-ups where your back and your legs are straight. I'm pretty flat-chested, I have to get really low before I touch the floor. On some days I'll feel a rush in the late afternoon. If I don't work out, I go into something that must be like withdrawal.

Before I left email came from an FBI agent—I also cover money laundering and terrorist financing—who normally didn't do email. He wanted to have lunch at a financial crimes conference in Florida. I typed *Yes*, but didn't hit send. *SIN* had no budget for Florida either. Going to this conference was a must and I couldn't go. The law enforcement presence was big. If I went missing, people would think I didn't rate.

There was some email chit chat. I needed him to tell me what happened there while leading him to believe I was going. I couldn't say yes to lunch then not show. Actually, I could. I'd call in sick the day before and he'd fill me in later. That was perfect. That was cheesy. Then there was the question of how much I could trust what he said.

He sent more messages while I was thinking of Doris Morris again—thinking of her as being far away when she was across the street. I saw a rainswept highway and a car with Doris and a half dozen people from the call center packed inside. They were singing like Camp Fire Girls when the driver skidded on a patch of wet asphalt, ran off the road and the car rolled over. It was still rolling when I told the FBI agent I had to go.

I scanned my badge and went down a staircase to the women's locker room. I noticed someone next to my locker. At first it wasn't Doris, then it was. I was expecting the person in the photo she sent me, where she was standing in a parking lot in pink tights. She didn't look at all like that. She was completely naked.

"Kay. We meet again."

"I don't think we've met before. In the flesh, that is."

I thought about shaking her hand. She smiled. She just phoned me, but for some reason I didn't expect her to be there. I opened my locker, then looked at her again. It was really her. Still naked. She was very pale. I was drawn to the hair peeking out of her armpits, darker than the hair on her head. I couldn't tell about her pubic hair—I refuse to say *kitty*. She'd shaved it.

I began to think of all the times I'd seen people with nothing on. After my kids most of them were men. But then there were all those women in locker rooms. That made me think of all those calls Doris made to me, when I stood naked in my apartment with nothing but a phone in my hand, when it was the crack of dawn and she was in debt collection mode. What day was this? Was I really supposed to be here?

Doris put on a t-shirt, no sports bra. She smiled. "Do you want to go to one of them group workouts upstairs, Kay?"

"No."

"You wanna work out with just me?"

"No."

"Why not?"

"I warm up on the treadmill. See you later."

I left my locker door open and stood behind it so Doris couldn't see me getting changed. I had her call center phone voice in my head still. This same person now goes to my health club where she could see me naked five times a week. When I thought about it yesterday, her moving here seemed like a break. Just don't join my gym.

There's an unwritten rule in this business—a

best practice, an immutable law or a cliche—that says you're not supposed to get personally involved in a story. Good reporters, so this story goes, maintain their objectivity, keep their prejudices to themselves and don't take sides. Then in the 1960s—before my time— there was the New Journalism, where if you *didn't* become involved in the story, some people called you a sellout. That's what I heard.

People fret about this. Some say it's bullshit, some say it's not while others acknowledge that times have changed, that it all depends on the kind of story you're writing, the time, the place and a thousand other things. Then they turn the page. If I've turned the page, why do I still fret about it?

Sometimes it's part of what arouses the fear that even when I'm good, I'm not good enough. Some people say, "Don't worry, Kay, you're a pro." Others don't go that far. This is an industry that loves to congratulate itself as much as it does flagellate itself, where they give each other awards one day and stab each other in the back the next. There are guidelines and codes of conduct that some news organizations support as proof of their rectitude while others don't. There's a game of one-upmanship that doesn't end, which has made me bitter. People get really possessive about *their* beat and *their* reporting.

I also tend to fight with editors. It's not anything I plan, but when I think they're wrong, I tell them, and I think they're wrong a lot. I don't think I go looking for trouble. Other people say, "Kay, you go looking for trouble way too much."

But it feels good to write a story that catches an official committing fraud or abusing the public trust. It feels horrible when you get a story wrong. I've done both. For the most part, you're only as good as your sources and it often feels like you're really doing someone else's thing.

Sometimes reporters can seem a little like cops or lawyers. Most people hate you until they think they need you. I've never covered a war but I once dated a war correspondent when we briefly worked at the same newspaper. He was brave and heroic. He was also addicted to conflict and violence and was always going off to a war, he couldn't stay away. It ended quickly enough but because of that, I can't say I've never had sex with a colleague or a source. Geoff was kind of a colleague, even if our relationship didn't depend on work. He could have approached me in a bar, or I could have approached him, and the outcome would have been the same.

Meanwhile you don't need a license to do this job like you would if you sold hot dogs on the street and even though J-schools have taken over, it's more a craft than a profession. Now there's web journalism where anything goes and there's no time to stop and think. There's more opportunity to throw caution to the winds which is hard to ignore, especially if there's money to be made. You could exercise caution. You could throw it to the winds again. This is just my opinion. What's happened to me doesn't define anything or anyone.

I kind of backed into this. I didn't come with the idealism that a lot of people do. Later I became idealistic until I lost my idealism. Over the years this became a job, nothing more, nothing less, but it was also a way of life. Sometimes I got out-hustled because I had kids. For a while I was going to daycare twice a day, picking up the kids and dropping them off. Rod was sick a lot as a child and I stayed home with him. Once I got fired for that. There was nothing I could do.

Now there's the student loan story and again I'm

reminded that my daughter and I are part of that whether I like it or not. We're only a small part, that's the thing. There are millions of people who could be trapped in these loans for decades. I don't want to fret about being part of this story if that keeps me from telling it. If I could write something that somehow helps other people, it's worth the effort. Knowing Leenie, she won't want to touch this. She could surprise me, though.

I got on a treadmill upstairs. It's a like conveyor belt you run on, an absurd contraption. Even though it's flat, it's like a hill you have to climb, even if you don't raise the platform. On a panel in front of you there's a button where you dial up numbers from low to high. The higher the number, the faster the belt turns and the faster you run.

It's perfect for people who don't like to exercise. Because you don't go anywhere, it's easier to stop than it would be if you ran laps around a track. You could buy a treadmill and never set foot on it but trick yourself into thinking you're getting in shape because you live with it. I knew somebody like that. The treadmill was the biggest object in her apartment. She didn't use it.

I dialed it up to 28, then 33. That's walking. I nudged it up to 38. That's still walking. I broke into a run at 44 which is really slow, a 12-minute mile, then hit the stop button after a couple minutes. I wasn't into it. I couldn't run another step.

I went up to the next floor and waited by the workout studios for people to drift in. During the week there were at least six workouts from about five o'clock on. On Saturday there were only two. Fewer people came.

I first came on Saturday after the last time I saw Geoff. Everybody there seemed newly single, divorced, separated, new in town or somehow unattached, you could just tell. That group was nearly all women. It's like an unofficial singles group of people who don't always identify as being single. I don't know what it is, but it seems like everything you've worked for, everything you do all day prevents you from having a partner.

gets in the way of being anything but single. I'm not describing this right, but there you are. Instead of going out, being with somebody you love—or like—you're at the gym, waiting for the burn.

There were two workout studios side by side on the third floor with a sign-up sheet on the door. Butt Breaker took place in one, Bhangra Boogaloo in the other. Butt Breaker combined aerobic exercise with hand weights and used to be called Booty Boot Camp. It wasn't like a military boot camp but let the customers have their fantasy. In the spring they switched from hand weights to body bars and called it Bun Burner. It was all tension and stress even if it's limited to certain muscle groups. It burned your buns.

Bhangra Boogaloo was ethereal, spiritual, but not unlike an Indian greatest hits dance workout. Aditi, the instructor, was born in Seattle but her family was from India and she started this workout in her father's garage based on Indian dance. Then she turned it into a business—like Leenie's shoe refurbishing business. She takes this workout act on the road. She's like an Indian Richard Simmons. Or an Indian Jillian Michaels.

I love this workout but it's more dance than aerobic and I'm a terrible dancer. I can run, I can jump but I can't dance. A couple times I tried and left before it was over. I came back and watched.

I was watching now, trying to figure out which workout Doris would go to. I wanted to talk to her, just not today. I was sure she'd pick Bhangra Boogaloo. It was easier. I went for Butt Breaker.

The serious people have already done another workout. The instructor is West Indian and goes by the name Miss Ann. A month after an appearance on *Sweat TV*, she's already sweating from the 10-mile bike ride she takes to get here. She is ripped. She is not friendly. She doesn't call attention to herself and makes the same announcement: this is *your* workout. Don't worry about what the person next to you is doing. Concentrate on *your* performance.

But people look to see who's doing what. Is this chick next to me keeping up? Is she doing real push-ups or girly push-ups? Along with estrogen, women produce testosterone, too, similar to men, even if it's different. I can feel *something* coursing through the veins of the woman in front of me, the woman behind me and the ones beside me. Once when we were on the floor doing crunches, I got a stitch in my side. I went rigid and rolled over, I couldn't move. Miss Ann got in my face screaming, "Aw, do you want a *cookie?* Do you want a *cupcake?* Do you want a *cheeseburger?*" I don't know why she picked on me. I usually crush it.

Miss Ann was just closing the door when Doris pushed it open. She stood in the last space at front. Baggy shorts, baggy t-shirt, no bra. I was one row behind her. She turned around but didn't see me. When the group split into two sections we were in the same one.

Half the group lined up along one wall, the other half against the opposite wall. Miss Ann started with interval training, where you run to the wall on the other side, then jog back, run, then jog back. That was the first 15 minutes. There was no music. All you'd hear was 40 feet hitting the floor. At the ten-minute mark, people start to slow down. I didn't think I was going to make it because of what I ate.

Before I left the office, a cleaning lady came by and said, "Here, you're too skinny," and put a box with eight cannoli on my desk. They're like sweet dough wrapped around creamy, processed sugar. In certain parts of New York, they're considered a delicacy, a fetish or as common as bottled water, I wouldn't know. I don't know what I was thinking when I ate them. Actually, I was hungry because I forgot to eat. After I finished the last one, they felt leaden.

Sometimes I have food fantasies when I run. I tried to conjure some that would stave off the cannoli that were roiling my gut. I have fantasies about healthy food. Snow peas. Cottage cheese. I love cottage cheese after a workout chased with milk. Cheese and crackers. New England clam chowder on a December day with sour dough bread. A turkey club sandwich on rye, hold the bacon, with healthy fries and boysenberry juice. Pasta of all kinds with red sauce. Cannoli are out of character.

Or whole wheat pizza. I thought whole wheat pizza didn't make any sense until Leenie found a place that made pizza with wheat crust that was better than white dough crust. Sometimes we had pizza night three nights a week. Some nights I'd race home before Leenie to get to the leftover slices, usually two from an eight-slice pie. Once I got there and she was eating the leftovers with one of her shoe customers. "Sorry, Mom," she said. "This is a business lunch." It was almost midnight.

I was trying to run to this, like it was a brass ring at the other end of the floor. I ran to visions of the pizza and the aroma. It wasn't working. I had all this food in my head but the cannoli in my gut were about to come up. They were halfway there. It was like an out-of-body experience—those cannoli would be out of my body and on the floor. It wasn't going to be like a tide of sudsy water leaking out of a washing machine, it was going to be a flood. I thought I'd better stop. Pull over, drop out. There was another ten minutes of interval training left. Tonight I wasn't going to make it.

I heard what sounded like a bucket of water splashing on the floor behind me. Twenty pairs of feet slowed down, then stopped. I turned around. That sound was Doris Morris throwing up. My stomach settled down.

Doris was on her knees coughing. It was like somebody threw lumpy yellow paint across the floor. People looked away. The energy started to go out of the room. A few just left. Others were waiting around for somebody to come with a mop. There was an ick factor that drove more people away. If this workout is the highlight of your Saturday evening, you're not happy. People were saying, "What did she have for lunch?" I couldn't feel the cannoli. They could have been in someone else's body. They were gone.

I was going to go over and ask Doris if she was ok. I kept my distance as she was talking to Miss Ann, who had to wait around until someone came to clean the floor. Then I thought, why stick my nose in this? It was my chance to get away.

I went back to the treadmill. I couldn't do Doris tonight, it didn't matter why, I just couldn't. I started at a walking pace, dialed it up to the 70s, then stopped after ten minutes. I couldn't run any more tonight. My body was telling me to stop. Being one more person with nothing to do on a Saturday brought me here. I was thinking about a woman who got on a treadmill next to me last week. After she ran for about five minutes she said, "I think my knee hurts," then fell like a sack of soybeans.

The woman's locker room was deserted. During the week there's somebody who gives out towels. She wasn't there. The people who constantly clean the place weren't there either. I wasn't sweating that much and thought about leaving without a shower. Then I got out of my clothes. The trip uptown was just too long and the water pressure here was better than at my apartment.

The shower was at the back, down the end of a long, narrow flight of stairs. It's wet and slippery and the steam dims the lights. Turn the lights off and it would remind you of a dungeon. I've been waiting for somebody to fall. Flip flops don't help. I'm always in my bare feet and going slow.

I heard voices. There was a commotion beyond the bottom of the stairs, where you turn left to get to the showers. They have shower stalls but no doors, just curtains. It got louder. I slowed down when I started to slip on what felt like a puddle of shampoo. I forgot to bring my own. I thought about turning back when I heard a voice I recognized.

There were three naked women at the last stall, two with their backs to me. The other was Doris. It looked like she was trying to leave. These other two were blocking the way and pushing her back. They were all talking at once while the showers drowned them out. The one with red hair pushed Doris down. Her ass made a smacking sound when it hit the floor. She tried to get up, they pushed her down again.

"You're a fat bitch," said the redhead.

"We don't like it when fat bitches fuck up our workout," said the other, whose hair was white. I don't think it was white because of her age. She seemed fairly young.

The redhead turned around and looked at me, then went back to Doris. "If you can't do the workout, don't come."

Doris tried to get up again when her feet went out from under her. The redhead started to kick her and I almost lost my footing when I grabbed her by the arm. "What do you think you're doing?"

"Mind your business."

"No, what are you doing?"

Her face was flushed, pale, blending with the steamy haze. "Oh, so you like it when she comes here and tosses her cookies," said the one with white hair.

The redhead threw out her arms and looked at me. "She threw up in *my workout*."

"And *my* workout," said the white-haired one. "The only reason I'm here is for this specific workout. Now I gotta wait a whole week."

Doris was on her feet, bending over with her hands on her knees. "Ok—I know how expensive it is to come here."

"If your company is paying for this, I don't think you do. I'm paying 100% out of pocket. I'm like her, I'm here for this workout—and you fucked it up!"

Doris was panting. "I wasn't trying to throw up— I was...if I knew this was gonna happen...I woulda gone home."

"You still came."

"And you're still here."

They were still really mad. I couldn't remember

seeing either of them before.

Doris pointed toward the ceiling. "Whyncha go do another work out."

The redhead pointed at Doris. "First, I should smack you for throwing up. Second—"

"What'd you say to me?"

I stepped between them, pushing away Doris and pushing away the redhead as my hands slipped from their sweaty tits. I didn't speak, I just pushed.

I was on a dry patch of floor, they stood in water. They were slipping and backed away. Then they wrapped their towels around their waists. It was like they said, Oh, let's be modest.

I'd never seen this kind of behavior before in any health club. These two women, who were still naked from the waist up, were probably high-end corporate citizens. Maybe not the highest of the high end, but membership wasn't cheap. Still, this was not how people at this place behaved. They were mad because they were deprived of their workout. Fine. It was an accident—I guess. Was it worth getting this mad?

They went back up the stairs to the locker room. I followed, calmly. The two women were holding their towels in their hands and were standing around Doris's locker. The redhead was closest to me. The one with white hair had a tattoo below her butt cheek that said:

Secret Tattoo

I saw it coming up the stairs.

I dropped my towel. Doris didn't have hers. We were all naked again. I decided I was going to physically intervene if I had to. I focused on the redhead. Doris opened her locker.

"What do you expect me to do," Doris said, "write

you a check?"

"Yeah," said the redhead, "you could write me a check."

Doris took a breath, then exhaled. She looked up, she looked down. "So how much am I writin you a check for?"

"Let's make it half the monthly membership fee."

Doris had her locker door open. She reached for her handbag, got out her check book and flipped it open.

"Who do I make this out to?"

The two women looked at each other. Before either one could reply, Doris threw her checkbook in her locker and slammed the door.

"On second thought, go fuck yourself."

"Excuse me?" said the red head.

"Whatever happened, I didn't do nothing on purpose. You ain't holdin me up for this."

The women looked at each other. For a second I thought the redhead was going to smack Doris. "This isn't over," she said. They slammed empty locker doors as they walked away.

I watched them go and wondered who they were. No doubt they worked near here. I could see them next week, or the week after. Or on the street.

I was standing around, trying to remember what plans I had for tonight. They didn't include this. Doris was putting on her bra, then stopped as if to see who was watching. Maybe I should hang out with Doris tonight after all.

She looked very different with her clothes off, like she stepped into a costume when she got naked. There were rolls of fat around her waist, two rolls were separated by her navel, there was more at the place where the white-haired woman had her secret tattoo.

To say she had poor muscle tone missed the point. There was something about her that sagged. After I'd noticed that, I felt something sensual about her that I couldn't locate. When it left the room I wanted to grab myself by the scruff of the neck. This was Doris, who I wanted to kill when she called at the crack of dawn.

"Are you ok?" I said.

She put on her socks. "I'm ok."

"What are you going to do?"

"About what?"

"It's like they were trying to extort money from you. What was that about?"

"I got fat-shammed. So what? They do it on TV."

"I don't have a TV."

Doris gave me an incredulous look. "You don't have a TV? Are you, like, antisocial?"

"It's a way to save money."

"It's cutting yourself off from the human race if you ask me."

Doris's rapacious debt collector voice was on. It echoed in the locker room the way her conversational voice didn't.

"Do you want to talk to management about this? I'll go with you."

Doris lowered her voice. "Would that be the guy in the black suit that sits by the door?"

"I'm not sure who you mean."

She was looking down at the floor as she pushed her clothes into her back pack. "If it's him, I don't."

"Are you ok?"

"I think that one chick just grazed my face when she kicked me. Doesn't hurt." Doris touched her cheek. "I did the gym, now I'm goin home. It's a long way to Queens and I'm still gettin the hang of the trains. We'll talk later. Thanks."

"Let's go out and get a drink. Who were those two women?"

Doris was dressed. My shorts got tangled up as I stepped out of them. I fumbled with my shoe laces, then tripped on them and almost fell to the floor. When I looked up, she was gone.

I got changed and wandered around to see if those two women from the shower were still here. The person at the front desk didn't know who I was talking about when I described them. I wondered if they were ex-military. I was pretty sure I'd never seen them before. If they skipped next Saturday, I skipped the Saturday after and they skipped the week after that, it would be a month before I saw them. I wondered how serious they'd be about trying to collect on what they thought Doris owed them. They couldn't be serious, though. I wondered if they were a couple.

I meandered a little. Went to the coffee dive next door, bought a latte. I thought about buying a pair of wrist bands that keep the sweat off your hands. I wasn't going to sleep well tonight because I didn't get a good workout. I lapsed into a mood—it's not really a mood—where I wondered where Geoff was. I sent him an e-mail in the morning. There was no reply but it didn't bounce back. Part of me was angry that he didn't answer, part of me was relieved. Describing it is futile. That didn't keep me from trying to describe it to myself.

I stood by the doorway of the gym for a while before I left. I almost gave the treadmill another try but they'd be closing soon. The street didn't exactly beckon. I wondered where all the people from the workout went after they left. They seemed to disappear. I wondered how many of them had crappy water pressure in their apartments.

Then, walking up Whitehall Street, this tiny, two

block-long street that turns into Broadway across from where I work, there was Doris, walking ahead of me. She was moving slowly. I hesitated, then caught up with her.

"Doris..."

She looked me up and down. "You still here?"

"That was a pretty cryptic exchange we had at the end."

"The end of what?"

"Want a drink?"

Doris nodded. "Ok. I know a place."

"How can you know a place? I thought you just moved here?"

"I still know a place."

Broadway veered to the right and began to rise. We went catty corner across the street to a door and down a flight of stairs, then to another door. She walked ahead of me and went straight to the women's room in the back. You couldn't see it from where we came in.

I sat at the bar across from a big mirror. There were only two other people. The fixtures were old and made of dark wood that was scratched and marred. There were two TVs. While I waited, I had this strange sense that I couldn't remember what Doris looked like. Like if she walked by I wouldn't recognize her. She wouldn't recognize me. I imagined sitting alone for hours. A strange woman would sit down a few stools away. We'd sit for a long time. Then she'd lean over and say, "Kay, is that you?" I had no list of questions like I did for Mathias Fokker.

Doris came out wearing new make-up and a different smile than when we met, just different enough. I was thinking of the photo in the parking lot she e-mailed me. She didn't seem like the same person. She'd spruced up her curls.

We were two bar stools apart, trying to order a drink. I watched her in the mirror behind the bar as she primped her lipstick. Here's Doris Morris, the voice that haunted my kitchen phone, who didn't disclose her identity when she called but couldn't keep from saying her first and last name. She threw up in my workout and I found her just as she was being attacked in the shower.

Now she was going to do what—out herself as a disillusioned debt collector? Dish about this awful business but leave out everything that was important? Did she have something to be afraid of? I was trying to remember the time of year when Doris called most and the more I tried, the less I could recall. The weeks and months when it was only Doris calling and the times when it was a dozen others faded away and came back. I spent a lot of time wondering how to make those calls stop. She moved over to the stool next to me.

"Well, it looks like this was fate," Doris said.

"What?"

"Us being here."

"I don't believe in fate."

"Oh, it was fate, alright."

"It's a coincidence because we work in the same part of town. Not fate."

"No, fate, totally. What're you drinking?"

We decided on red wine. The first sip was a gulp, then I started to sip slowly.

"So who were those women?"

"You already asked me that."

"I'm asking again."

Doris paused for a moment, like there was more than one answer and she was trying to pick the right one. "I don't know. I haven't been going there long enough to know people."

"I didn't recognize them," I said. "Did they know each other? At first I thought the ringleader was that redhead with the big...rack."

"We don't say *rack* where I come from, Kay. We say *tits*."

"What did those women say to you in the shower before I got there?"

Doris took a hit of wine. "Forget about them. Let's talk about what you say you wanna pick my brains over—the call center. I didn't sign any papers that say I can't talk about the job."

"Great. Tell me about the call center. When did you start there?"

She pushed her curls off her face. "I kind of don't know where to begin. Different people have different jobs."

"Let's start with your job. How come you called me so much, but when I called Fedloan, it was never you that answered?"

Doris lifted her drink. "I could tell you a little bit about that now and more later. I want to get to know you better first."

"Fair enough." I stared into my wine glass. I glanced at Doris. She was staring into hers, too, like she was looking for something.

She looked at me. "Those two chicks in the locker room were like a posse, right?"

"Did you know them?"

"Us chicks at the call center in PA were like a posse, too. I'm the only one who quit of the ones I know. I mean, to tell you the truth, what happened in the shower makes me think of the stuff we did at the call center, only over the phone."

"Was harassing people part of the job?"

"Part of the job? You should see this place."

"That's what I want to hear about."

"Oh, you'll hear about it."

"Were you encouraged to threaten people?"

"Whaddia mean?"

"I think you know what it means, Doris. One customer service rep told me I'd go to jail if I didn't pay—that's illegal. Did they tell you to threaten people?"

Doris didn't reply, like she was still trying to figure out what she wanted to say. If she didn't know where to begin, we'd be here until they closed the place. I had no tape recorder, nothing to write with.

"I mean, I know how I sounded," she said, "when I phoned from the call center. Sometimes I told people they were gonna go to jail if they didn't pay. Really, the job made me crazy."

"I'm over a barrel on this, Doris. I'll take your word for it."

She gave me a look. I wanted to qualify that remark. I didn't want to put her off. I wanted her to open up.

"I mean, you should see what it's like there," Doris said. "We get threatened by the supervisors and the people that owe. I had supervisors tell me to do stuff we were told *not* to do when we got trained. But when you get on the floor at the call center, it's different and you go the way the wind blows. I had a supervisor say `Keep these people broke so they never get out of debt.'"

She looked up at the television. "People don't want to work at this place. There's openings right now, even with times as tough as they are. The job ad at the website says, '*Loan counselors answer inbound and outbound calls and initiate contact handling a variety of complex issues.*'"

"Wait, you're a loan counselor? That's your job title?"

"I say I'm collecting debt, no matter what they say the job is. In my opinion, a loan servicer and a debt collector are in the same game, even if a collection agency is a different animal."

"How does the process it start?"

"I'd say what you're asking about starts with delinquency, and it's *so easy* for a loan to go delinquent. All you have to do is miss one payment—just one—or be a day late. You still have a while to pay up before you get reported to the credit bureaus. On the other hand, you might get reported right away."

She laughed. "But you'd be surprised what some people do next. They'll say, 'Oh, so now I'm a proven loser, why pay *anything* since I gotta get my nails done.' Then they act like this is gonna go away if they wait long enough. After 270 days of non-payment, the borrower is in default. The loan goes to the Department of Education's Default Resolution Group which is really a private company. But not always. I don't know what they do with it. Then we get it back—usually. There's stuff I'm leaving out."

"What stuff?"

She took a drink. "Stuff I can get later. There's guidelines we learn when we're trained. We follow them. We break them. We call borrowers who default at least three times a month. But the federal government only pays Fedloan about 50 cents a month per defaulted loan—that's what I heard—so we only call the minimum. Loans that aren't being repaid go into different categories—like forbearance and in-school deferments. They all have different fees. Fedloan gets paid more to keep loans out of default. That's why you got called a lot. You weren't in default yet."

"How do they train you to do calls?"

"Sometimes we're on a leash. Sometimes there's

no leash. One supervisor says, 'Get the money, don't get played. That's the slogan. Get that tattooed to your arm.'"

"Did you get the tattoo?"

Doris rolled up her sleeves. There were no tattoos. "The supervisor that told us 'Don't get played' got fired, but I kept on doin like he said. So I'm on the phone yelling at a borrower and the new guy comes over and says 'My office!' We get there and he goes 'Mean people suck! If I catch you screaming at a borrower again, you're gone!' I told him that's how the last guy wanted it—and by the way, I'm fed up with my working conditions. He goes, 'That's not a valid complaint. Everybody at Fedloan is fed up.' He quit. I was back yelling at borrowers."

"Was it ok with the next supervisor?"

Doris rearranged her curls. "You also gotta do the math on the borrower's loans when you're talking to them. I flunked math in high school, always, always. We get complex issues at the call center, alright."

"So what are the complex issues?"

Doris gave me a funny look. "*You* already know how complicated this is right? How long have I been talkin to you for?"

I took another hit from my wine glass. "I'm really clueless. Part of me is resisting this because in my heart I think my daughter should be dealing with this, not me."

Doris took a swig. "Here's what they expect. You're supposed to counsel the customers into making successful repayments. What's a successful repayment? I don't really know. What they *don't* want is call escalation. That's when somebody gets pissed off and says, 'Gimme your supervisor!' That happens when I can't answer your payment questions, advise you about repayment options, loan forgiveness and consolidations or forbearance—you're mad cause you ain't hearin what you wanna hear and I get in trouble."

"So you're giving financial advice."

Doris laughed her call center laugh. "People ask, 'What are my legal rights?' I tell them to pay your freakin loan and you won't have to worry about your damn rights. It's not always that simple, though. You can do like we say and still get fucked up. I don't tell people I'm a lawyer and I don't say I'm not. But it sounds enough like legal advice so that some people think I am."

"Where does it say you're a loan counselor?"

"There's all kinds of job titles. Look at the job openings on the website for loan counselors—another word for call center chicks. If you ask me, they have us givin financial advice and you get it from somebody with only a high school diploma or a GED cause that's who they hire."

"How come?"

"They're only paying the minimum wage. Who that's qualified to give financial advice would work for that?" Doris took another hit of wine. "It's almost impossible to get a raise. I bet they hire people with no education because management thinks they'll be stuck in the job and can't leave."

I was nursing my wine. Doris downed hers and ordered another. "I worked different hours and they hot seat the work stations. That means somebody else uses it before me and after me. One day I came in and the chair was completely broke. I'm in that chair all day. They wouldn't fix it. Just thinking about it makes my butt hurt."

"Why did you leave?"

Doris didn't seem to hear. "You don't have no say

over who you're calling," she said. "I heard they're thinking about training reps for certain loans, like some would only do borrowers with professional school loans—doctors, lawyers—some regular college, some community colleges, some for-profit colleges. That was the rumor."

"What's a for-profit college?"

Doris drew back. "You don't know what a for-profit college is?"

"I've heard of them. Should I find out more?"

She shrugged. "Don't make no difference to me. That just means you don't know shit about higher ed."

Doris downed her drink. "Think about it. Let's say you got $30,000, $70,000, sometimes $300,000 in student loans spread over a bunch of private and federal loans. You've had these loans for five, ten, *twenty years*. You've been in and out of forbearance, when you don't have to pay. Then years later you owe more than when you started because when you're in forbearance they keep charging interest. Or you miss a payment by *one day* and they add fees. You're desperate, at the end of your rope. Who you gonna call? Your loan servicer. Who you gonna get? Somebody with a GED makin the minimum wage. Do you think I *really* wanna help with your freakin problem? Do you think I even *know how* if I just started last month or last week and I'm gonna be gone in 90 days? I'm thinking about my supervisor, not you. I wanna get *you* off the freakin phone while I'm watchin the clock. Although I had a supervisor who was as fed up as me."

"Really? I'd like to talk to that person."

Doris lifted her glass. It was empty. "What you need is an expert. Like a lawyer. But if the lawyer don't know student loans, it ain't helpin. And you'll still pay."

I thought about my balance on the PLUS Loans.

I wasn't sure what it was because the fees and interest kept driving it up. It was going higher while I was sitting here talking to Doris. I thought of all the advice I got from the call center reps. It was never the same advice. It was rarely good advice. I didn't always have my story straight. Leenie was on the West Coast with parts of the story I didn't have. I'm an inveterate note-taker but I didn't take many notes on these calls because I already felt defeated. I could be fully clothed and feel naked when Doris called.

And I saw her naked. It was disarming. She was 20 pounds overweight but seemed comfortable in her own skin, assuming I can jump to that conclusion.

It made me think about my own skin. Men have told me, "You're so beautiful Kay, but there's something inhuman about the way you're beautiful." I don't know how much veiled hostility there is behind a remark like that—a lot, probably. With some guys, it was a come-on when we met, with others it was a dig at me as it was ending. You'd think a man who thought I was beautiful would be happy about that. Instead it often seems to make them resentful. I've heard the theories and explanations. I'll never understand it.

Doris's voice startled me.

"So Kay, if you're so inarested in my story, how come you don't ask nothin about me?"

"I'm sorry, what?"

"You don't ask about me. You don't ask how's my job, how's where I'm living, how's dating..."

"I'd ask about your personal life when it's appropriate."

"What's wrong with now?"

I took another look at this person who was assaulted in the locker room of my health club an hour or two ago and now wants to talk about dating. This was a little incongruous. I almost pointed this out.

"Ok, Doris, I'll bite. How's dating?"

"I'm not really dating."

The bartender refilled her glass. I waited. I was feeling light-headed.

"Is there something you want to discuss about that?" I said.

"I'm looking for advice and thought maybe you got some. Where do you meet people at? Who are you dating?"

"Right now? I don't know if what I'm doing could be called dating."

"What's it called?"

"I haven't thought of a name."

We sat, looking in the mirror behind the bar. I'd glance at her, she'd glance at me. I imagined Doris as somebody who had another life outside the call center or her new job in the word processing pool, one she couldn't wait to get back to when her shift ended. I thought of her as a singer in an all-girl band. I imagined them struggling to find a place to rehearse, looking for abandoned factories in Allentown or Bethlehem. Then finding a gig was a struggle. They had to drive between road houses and strip joints with a U-Haul trailer that took them into Maryland and West Virginia or Ohio and Indiana. She left PA. I wondered what she left behind.

I was comparing her to my daughter. When I did, I saw somebody with no band, no pursuit outside of the job she didn't want, nothing else in her life. I don't know what Leenie did when she wasn't working in the restaurant. She was being thwarted by things beyond her control while I was 3000 miles away on this bar stool.

Doris could have some unusual talent but if it was something she didn't act on, the world wouldn't know. I imagined her at the call center, shutting down her workstation, going home and parking herself in front of the television. I figured Doris was five years older than Leenie. Or six. I was fooling with numbers again, this time about Leenie's age. Without my calculator.

Doris slammed her wine glass on the bar.

"Damn it, Kay, you're supposed to ask how I'm doin! Am I happy, am I sad, can't you at least say that? What the hell kind of a reporter are you anyway? And I never heard of that newspaper you work at, neither."

"Doris—you're on edge. No one would blame you after what happened. But there are some things you have to explain. I wasn't expecting a conversation about dating."

"No, I know what you're thinkin. You think I'm some fat chick from PA, huh, who can't get a date and when it comes to dating I'm worthless, huh?"

"I don't think that, Doris."

"You don't have to say nothing. I know you."

"No, you don't. I'm not a big city girl, either. I was born in Bucyrus Falls, Montana, population 2400. Give or take."

"Never mind, Kay. You're gonna meet *my* posse, then we'll see."

"Who?"

"My call center girls are coming here from PA for a visit tomorrow, so tell you what. Let's meet up then and you'll get to hear their story, not just mine."

"Tomorrow?"

She wrote her phone number on an envelope. "Here's where you find me. Let's firm it up in the morning. Stella Recker is coming. I want you to meet her."

"Where we going to meet?"

"Radio City Music Hall. Phone me, but wait for us at the front door. You can make it, right?"

"Of course, Doris. I'll walk you to the subway."

"Don't bother. We take different trains."

I watched her go. I couldn't reconcile Doris's appearance with her voice on the phone. I don't know if this was an illuminating detail or if I'm sweating the small stuff. We *did* take different trains. Although if she took the A train to 42nd Street and caught the E train there, that'd be faster than if she got the E at the World Trade Center.

I didn't have my reporter's hat on. I wore my student loan borrower hat, which is so heavy you can't always keep your head up, especially late at night when you're tired and had too much to drink. The scene in the shower might not have been isolated. But we broke the ice. And I was supposedly meeting these call center people. That'd be a good get. I didn't expect to get that lucky.

I didn't ask why she left PA and came here. I wanted to let her mention it. I *could* get a more candid response if I asked her first. Or a more evasive one.

I walked to the subway and stopped. If I was meeting Doris tomorrow, I couldn't work on Sunday, which was tomorrow, when I had work to catch up on at the paper. I still owed my editor that story about multi-asset class trading. I hesitated, then went back to the office. This was turning into an all-nighter. If the hedge fund meeting was over, I could sleep in the conference room. I looked for Stella Recker on the internet. Nothing turned up.

Chapter Four

I hadn't been to Radio City Music Hall since Leenie was in middle school. I don't have an attachment to these landmarks like some people. Seeing it through a child's eyes was the landmark.

By then she didn't want to be seen *anywhere* with me. Trying to engage her was like watching home-made bread that won't rise. Over Christmas that year I said, "Come on, Leenie, let's go see the Rockettes, this'll be *fun.*" I kept thinking, *Goddam it, you're still a kid—act like it!*

She had a boyfriend in the eighth grade. One day I came home from work early and heard them in bed. I had my key in the apartment door, her bedroom was just inside the doorway. I didn't meet the kid she was doing it with for another few minutes.

I backed out of the apartment thinking I'd go to a bodega while they finished. I waited calmly for the elevator. When it came I ran down the hall and into Leenie's bedroom. I can't remember what happened next but when it was over they weren't in bed anymore and this kid was getting dressed in the hallway. That's where I threw his clothes.

Later I thought that catching her in the act made her more determined. Sex in middle school primed her for failure, I was convinced of it, even if it isn't true. I'm good at obsessing about things I can't change. There were times when I wanted to ask someone's advice about this and a lot of other things but didn't. I don't like to ask for help. I believe in self-reliance. Sometimes I wish there was something else to believe in.

I dropped out of college in Colorado when I got a reporter job at a newspaper. I was making money—who needs school? But several years later I met this guy, Ned, and got pregnant with my son Rod. Ned was basically a good guy but marrying him was a bad idea. If I've made bad decisions with men, they were still my decisions.

Leenie's loans were really my decision, too. She's gone but the debt remains, like I'll find it in the bathroom brushing its teeth. She said she'd reimburse me for the Grad PLUS payments but who knows when. The money she borrowed, which was supposed to make her life sublime, could actually make her poor. I thought I'd saved her from that kind of fate—even if I don't believe it fate—the day I hauled that kid out of her bed, but the jury's still out on that. It makes me want to throw things against the wall when I think about it, usually when it's 3AM. The walls are thin. I don't want to wake the neighbors.

Even if the loans were paid off in ten years, Leenie still spent the money on something that has almost no value. The payments would be money she couldn't use to rent an apartment, never mind buying one. She's not in a public service field so she can't get public service loan forgiveness. Leenie is attractive and smart but men would avoid her because of her debt. Her relationships would fail. The next thing she knows, she's pushing 40.

Kids? There won't be any because Leenie can't afford them unless she wants to be a broke parent raising broke kids. Then she'd get knocked up by some sketchy hipster guy who says, "Me be a parent? Isn't there an app for that?" Most likely there will be the two of us, fighting on one hand, still estranged on the other.

Part of me didn't want to chase the Doris story if

it involved Leenie and any editor would probably want to leave her in. They'd say "Kay, you can't just leave out Leenie and you're in this, too." I don't know how Leenie would react if she saw this in print. That made me think about how estranged we were. She could hate it with all her heart and things wouldn't be much worse.

I woke up in the conference room on the 23rd floor and was slow to get moving until I heard voices near the elevator. The hedge fund people were back.

I looked like I was dressed for a costume party— khaki cargo pants and a pullover with glittery black sequins. I stopped at my desk for some heels, then almost blew off Doris and went home. We went to the same gym. How did that happen?

And what am I doing on Sunday morning after working Saturday night? Rushing off to meet Doris Morris. After a sloppy workout and a night of furtive drinking, I was counting on her to deliver information I wasn't going to get anywhere else. Doris could be merely eccentric or flat-out crazy. That didn't mean her story was wrong.

I got off the train at 47th Street and Sixth Avenue. I paced around in front of Radio City Music Hall, which is near Times Square, for about five minutes. Then it seemed like 35. I left my watch at work and it felt like I was being stood up. And, yes, a cell phone might help me find them faster. I also thought about blowing them off again. I couldn't do that, though, if she was bringing people from the call center. What if they were all nuts? Even better. This is who the loan servicers hire to work these loans. They get paid with taxpayer dollars.

I was looking for a clock when I heard Doris's

laugh. Her laugh floated above the street noise, like it was coming from a talking billboard high above a highway outside the town she grew up in. Then I saw her on Sixth Avenue walking toward me.

"Kay! We finally found you!"

"How long have you been looking?"

Doris looked at her watch. "About ten New York minutes."

"We don't do New York minutes anymore."

Doris frowned. "How do you tell time?"

"We have our ways."

A bunch of women were standing near her, looking up.

"Now that we've seen the Statue of Liberty, I'd like to go for a ride on a double-decker bus," she said.

I frowned. "That's too touristy, Doris."

"We're tourists. Except me. I live here now."

I could pick out the ones she came with. They had these light green hats that were more like visors with crowns from the Statue of Liberty above the bill. They were sold on the street, in dollar stores and five-star hotels. Five women with these hats were squinting into the sky. This was the call center posse.

"So Doris, let's go somewhere and talk. You could introduce me to your colleagues."

"Oh, we're not staying."

"Where you going?"

"Atlantic City, wanna come?"

"I don't."

"I think you should come."

I looked at the women that were standing behind her. "You're kidding," I said. "Right?"

"We're not kidding, Kay. Do you want this story?"

"I want it."

"Let's go get it."

A woman with dark hair and sad eyes, about 5'7", the same height as Doris, stood next to her. Doris's blond curls were pulled back into a bun, this woman had straight bangs and hair that touched her shoulders. "I'm Stella," she said. "I'm driving and we gotta get a move on."

"We're illegally parked," said Doris.

Stella shrugged. "So? We're from out of state. If we get a ticket, they can't collect cause we won't pay."

"Money you can't collect is a bitch," said Doris.

"Don't they send you to a collection agency," I said.

Nobody replied. Doris didn't say much about who was coming. They were all from her call center, but she didn't say whether they worked the same shift, met in the break room, if they'd trained together or how long she'd known them. I'd learned a little more about student loan servicing. Fedloan started small decades ago with a few thousand student loans. Now they manage millions worth billions of dollars and have thousands of customer service reps. That's a lot of bricks in the wall.

I followed them to a fire hydrant on West 45th Street where Stella unlocked her car. The doors creaked like doors to a haunted house.

"It's a Ford Crown Victoria," Stella announced. "A 1996 with 150,000 miles. Two-tone, white side wall tires. Big back seat. Gets you there from PA."

"Did you get a parking ticket," I asked.

"No."

"Great. By the way, I wasn't planning on a trip to Atlantic City. I was hoping we'd sit down somewhere and talk. Let's do that, shall we?"

"We can talk in the car," Doris insisted. "Just as good."

"It's only about 100 miles down the New Jersey Turnpike," Stella added.

"Garden State Parkway," Doris corrected.

I coughed. "Doris, this isn't what we said."

She gave me a look. "Kay, do you want to hear what we have to say or not?"

"I want to hear it."

"So get in, girlfriend."

"Why Atlantic City?"

"It's a girly road trip. We're gonna gamble and have some laughs."

They climbed in. The back seat was large and the front was a bench seat, about the same size. There wouldn't be room for me if there was an arm rest or console. Stella got behind the wheel, Doris sat next to her. Next to Doris was the only place for me as the other three got in the back. That made six of us. Doris held what seemed like a small suitcase on her lap.

Stella pulled out before I closed the door. The car was riding low to the street. There was a shimmy in the front end.

"Yeah, Kay," Stella announced, "you don't wanna sit around at some tourist trap in Times Square when you can go to AC and gamble like a boss."

"I'm not a gambler," I said.

"We're gamblers," said a voice from the back.

"Well, I'm not."

"Sure you are," said Doris. "This student loan thing you're writtin sounds like a gamble to me."

"That's not a good comparison."

"Sure it is. What if the story don't work out? And anyways, we're not gonna be gone that long. Really, it's not that far."

Traffic was light. Stella was already on West 42nd Street and turned left toward the Lincoln Tunnel.

I tried to guess what time I'd get home tonight.

What looked like a roomy interior from the street quickly became cramped. They all seemed to have handbags or luggage.

"Did I introduce you around yet, Kay?"

"We skipped the formalities."

"Let's get formal. You know Stella, she's driving and that's Marge right behind you in the back."

"Can't see you Marge, but hi," I said.

"And that's Peg next to her."

"Can't really see you either, Peg."

"And next to Peg there's Margot."

Peg said hi. Margot waved. Margot had stringy brown bangs, but it looked like the hair at the back of her head was a different color. Her hoop earrings jangled. Peg was just over my shoulder. I couldn't see Marge. She was right in back of me.

"Hey Kay, ever been to Atlantic City before," asked Doris.

"No. But I see New Jersey every day from my bedroom window."

"Then you came to the right place."

"How long does this trip take?"

"Will you stop, Kaaay?" Doris whined. "It's a couple of hours. Try to relax."

"Not enough room," someone said.

"Try. If that don't work, try harder."

Except for Peg, they were all fairly large ladies, around the same age as Doris—mid-20s to early 30s. Except for Doris, none seemed to have a weight problem. Except for Peg, I could see any of them riding on the back of a Harley with their arms around Sonny Barger or a stunt man from *Sons of Anarchy*. They seemed like biker chicks on the loose without their bikers. I had a note pad and a tape recorder in the pockets of my cargo pants. I hoped there was a spare tire in the trunk that wasn't flat.

There was a smell from the back seat.

I thought I heard Marge, who was right behind me, flicking a cigarette lighter. After the flicking stopped, smoke wafted over my shoulder. Cigarette smoke.

I was trying to decide whether or not to say something. Then it was a question of when. We were in traffic. There was nowhere to stop.

I cleared my throat. "Do you have to smoke?"

Silence followed. It was quiet enough to hear one of them working her cigarette lighter. "Yeah, I have to smoke," said Marge. "What's it to ya?"

"Can you roll down your window?"

"It's not gonna make no difference."

"Marge," said Doris. "Crack it some at least."

"Are you takin up with her," Marge demanded. "Cause she don't get to tell me when I can smoke."

"Just crack your window," I said.

The window was not cracked. This felt like the beginning of a 100-mile standoff. The smoke drifted to the front. There was a hammering sound coming from underneath the car.

Doris's suitcase seemed to be getting bigger. It was really a replica of a steamer trunk from 100 years ago. Small, but not really. It would slip around on her lap and she'd elbow me when it did. I looked at her fingernails, when her fingers were on the trunk, and at Stella's on the steering wheel. I don't get my nails done, but I observe what others do. They had nail treatments they probably did themselves, that looked several weeks old, where the polish receded from the edge of each nail and left a snowflake-shaped splotch in the center. I associated that with being a little girl when I was a little girl. Later I associated it with being impoverished. Stella had black polish. Doris had red.

I couldn't remember how much money I brought with me. I couldn't get into my pockets.

"Why are you going to Atlantic City?" I asked.

"Too late to turn back now," said Stella.

"There's a casino in Yonkers. It's closer. Why not go there?"

"There's a casino in Bethlehem, PA, too," Stella added. "We could go there if we wanted to stay local."

"You can smoke in Atlantic City," said Marge. Her words were mangled by a wracking, gurgling cough. "They tried to make rules against smoking but any time I go to a Trump casino, I always light up. Nobody ever told me to put out my cigarette. That Trump, he's lookin out for smokers if you ask me. I say God bless him."

"You can smoke in the PA casinos, too," Margot added, "but just certain parts. I think it's half the floor."

"My father said AC's the place to gamble," said Doris. "That's where the real gamblers go. The house odds are better."

"How does he know?" I asked.

"Doris's father is a big-time gambler," said Stella. "When he talks, you listen."

"How does he know the odds are better?"

Stella leaned over the steering wheel. "You're askin a lotta questions, Kay. Doris said you just wanna hear about the call center. Why you askin about her father?"

I had a list of questions in my pocket. I couldn't fish them out. I wanted to win them over first.

"Don't take any of this personally," I said. "It's more about the place you worked and these loans than it is about any one person."

"If you're asking *me* questions, then I'm in this,

too," Stella snapped. "What kinda questions are you askin?"

"Yeah," said Marge, "start us off with some idea."

I lowered the window and waved the smoke away. Wind whipped into the car. I rolled it back up. "For example, when you come in for your shift, how did you find out what calls to make? How did they decide who called which borrowers at the call center?"

"That's tricky," said Doris.

"Just thinkin about that makes me tired," said Stella. "And I do all the driving."

"So Stella," I said, "Could you have phoned me from the call center?"

"What difference does it make?"

"I wonder what the chances are."

"I'm sure I called you. If Doris called you, I called you."

"What makes you say that?"

"I don't know. Maybe I'm starting to remember your voice and how you talk."

"I find that hard to believe."

"Don't believe it then. You think I care about what you believe? I don't even know you."

"What's my name, Stella What's my last name?"

"You expect me to remember the name of every loser with a student loan?"

"They were for my daughter. I was just the co-signer."

Stella laughed. "So you co-signed for her and she gets to use the money, not you? That makes you a proven loser."

"She got you there, right Kay?" said Doris.

I thought about how far away Leenie was. I leaned over toward Stella. "Were you the one who called me a bitch?"

"What if I was?"

"Cause if anybody's a bitch, it's you."

"You callin *me* a bitch?"

Stella pulled over and as she hit the brake, Doris threw out her arms. "Whoa whoa whoa! Stop, the both of you! This is just a little trip. We'll do what Kay wants and tell some stories. We'll do what Stella wants, too, and hit the casino. Everybody gets what they want, ok? We good? Stella?"

"I'm *always* good," said Stella. "I'm one of the best."

The car stopped. I cracked my window. Another was cracked in the back. Stella moved back into traffic.

I lost it there for a minute. I thought I should apologize to keep things copasetic. I didn't. I didn't know how much patience I had for this. They could give me the silent treatment the rest of the way. If I bummed a cigarette from Marge, maybe I wouldn't seem like such a freak to her. I never smoked cigarettes. I'd be coughing my brains out.

Stella ran a red light, no one spoke. We were in the Lincoln Tunnel on the West Side of Manhattan. It was dark, bare light bulbs hung beside tiles on the walls that almost looked ancient. I thought about emperor's tombs, underground crypts and Native American burial grounds. New Jersey appeared when we came out the other side.

Doris shifted her trunk. I didn't want that goddam thing in my lap, but I didn't want to be left on West 45th Street either, watching an opening close like an off-off Broadway play no one would ever see again. If I was going to do this, I had to be riding in Stella's Crown Vic.

The posse wasn't talking. I was inhibiting them, I could tell. We were stopped in traffic. The engine sounded like a farm tractor.

"I met Doris at the gym the other day," I said.

"Don't tell me you're one of these health nuts," said Stella.

"What do you mean by *health nut*?"

"Doris wants to go on a diet," Margot announced. "I don't encourage her. It's hopeless, that's why. She'll never lose weight."

"Doris is allowed to try," said Peg, who had what looked like a pageboy haircut. She leaned over the seat and a flap of reddish blond hair fell across her face. "Are you still trying, Doris?"

Doris bit her fingernails and didn't answer right away. "I threw up at the gym when I was workin out with Kay."

Stella looked over the wheel at me. "Did she?"

"She did."

"No class, Doris."

Margot asked, "Did she apologize, Kay?"

"I would have apologized," said Peg.

"I heard you could pick up diseases in those kinda places," Stella clucked. "It happens."

Smoke wafted over my shoulder, then Marge's words. "Doris thinks she can lose her junk and be this tidy-ass skinny chick, then give everybody an attitude because she don't smoke."

"A person can quit smoking," Stella asserted. "I stopped."

"And you think you're all that cause you quit."

"You don't have kids, Marge. I did it for my kids, that's why."

"Excuse me?"

"One day I hadda make a choice between a pack of cigarettes or food for my kids," Stella said. "You think I hadda think twice?"

We were picking up speed. Outside the chaotic New Jersey landscape was going by. I had an answer in case they wanted to know more about what happened at the gym. Nobody mentioned it. I shouldn't have mouthed off to Stella. That wasn't buying me any love.

Stella leaned over the wheel. "What'd you do last night, Kay?"

"Worked at the office. I pulled an all-nighter."

"Were you by yourself?"

"Yup."

"Too bad you didn't bring a friend. You coulda had office sex. Ever have office sex, Kay?"

"No."

"Ever tape it on a cell phone?"

"I've never had office sex."

"So what do you write about? Besides student loans and debt collectors, which Doris said you didn't write about yet."

"I write about the securities industry, mainly the equity markets and foreign exchange, a little less about the bond markets and derivatives. I write about how stocks are cleared and settled after they're traded. That's the easiest way of putting it."

Stella peered over the wheel. "Are you talkin down to us, Kay? You think we're dumb or somethin?"

"Not at all. If you're wondering whether I have a stake in any of this, I don't. I'm just a trade press prol."

Doris laughed. "A trade press prol? What's that?"

"Is that something really technical," asked Stella.

"It's another way of saying my job sucks."

Stella laughed. "I'll say if you're workin on the weekend."

No one else laughed. Stella whipped past a truck. No one spoke. I watched the other cars go by and thought of the people in them. They could have been commuters in a car pool on their way to work, people who weren't exactly friends. They could be relatives who couldn't stand each other, on their way to visit another relative in a hospital that they'd never see again.

The mood would be tense, like the mood inside Stella's car. It went on through the industrial and post-industrial Jersey landscape that looked like one big conceptual art installation with highways thrown on top. I thought of smoke belching from exhaust pipes. I thought of the smoke in the car. Marge coughed. Margot hacked. It got quiet. I tried to think of something to say. I couldn't interview them here. I'd have to wait.

I'd written about trade data for years, focusing mainly on Wall Street. It had been a long time since I'd focused on people. There was little demand for that even though trade data was created by real people who massaged it, parsed it, stored it, anguished over it and were secretive about it.

That didn't mean their private lives couldn't be sensational. A few years ago, I was at a party with some reference data honcho when he did something really lurid and sociopathic. He became a different person after that. People still talk about it. But it didn't concern data. His ex-wife, who I'd met once, called me with a story about him that was sick, criminal, but lived outside of data. I asked her if she'd go on the record. She hung up. Years ago, working for some daily newspaper, I would have been crazy for a story like that. But I was struggling to get my arms around data. Anything else was a distraction I didn't want.

"So who here is married," I said.

"Who's married," said Stella incredulously. "Who the hell came here to talk about that?"

Doris picked her nose. "That's getting away from the call center thing, Kay."

"So I'm with somebody new," Margot announced. "But you all knew that."

Doris turned around. "I didn't know. Who?"

"Shhh, not now."

"C'mon, Margot!"

"Kay's here. I don't want to talk about it in front of her. She's a stranger."

"Tell me who! A guy or a chick?"

"Ok, I'll whisper." Doris, Marge and Peg all leaned in. Their voices dropped to a sigh. Stella ignored them. The car was rumbling as it hit a bumpy patch in the highway. I was trying to eavesdrop, then straining to keep my head up, suddenly feeling like I couldn't stay awake. It wasn't late. It was the middle of the day. There was a hum coming from the road. It faded away as I was nodding out.

Next month would be November. Last night I dreamed that my kids would be home for Thanksgiving even though I knew I wouldn't see them. I don't think they call my apartment *home* anymore. That was a dream I had to stop dreaming.

Soon I was asleep. I had a dream about a Thanksgiving dinner a long time ago and far from here. The dining room table was in Missouri, not far from the Arkansas border where I lived with my son Rod, Leenie and Leenie's father. Instead of a turkey there was a giant sleeping pill on a platter waiting to be carved. It was white and shiny, the biggest pill ever. Leenie's father didn't want to carve it. Leenie tried to lick it and her father hit her. I hit him back. There was a big ruckus and after it was over, he refused to carve the sleeping pill. I refused to sleep with him. None of this really happened but in the dream it seemed so vivid.

Rod helped me carve it. He was only a little boy. He put his hands on the sleeping pill that was the size of a 50-pound tom turkey. I couldn't get a fork into it and didn't even try the knife, it kept rolling around until it bounced off the platter like a beach ball. Rod tried to catch it but it slipped away, like a bowling ball that ran into a gutter and missed all the pins. Because I dreamed I was back in Missouri, I didn't know I'd fallen asleep in Stella's car.

The pill was rolling toward Rod and me. It rolled in slow motion. Then it came faster. I rolled down a hill, it rolled after me. We rolled like Jack and Jill rolling down the hill and it went on and on like a rhyme with no end. The sleeping pill was chasing me. It rolled forever. I don't know where Rod went. I called to him. He didn't answer.

My dreams have commercials. The dream stopped and the car commercials began—they were unrelenting. There was one for Midas Mufflers, one where the Geico gecko spoke through a ventriloquist that sat on his lap. I didn't know where I was until the dream began again and we were at a Walmart outside of Sikeston, Missouri near Interstate 55, the first Walmart built outside of Arkansas. We were arguing over what turkey to get. Then after we decided, the turkey we wanted was trying to escape. We chased it down the frozen food aisle. Then I was alone and it was chasing me. The turkey was bearing down on me like it wanted *me* for Thanksgiving dinner. When I ran out to the parking lot it was getting closer. I couldn't find the car. Then when I found it I couldn't find the keys. The turkey was on top of me in the Walmart parking lot, about to take a bite out of my face. I was trapped. My son was gone.

I opened my eyes. It wasn't a Thanksgiving turkey or a sleeping pill chasing me, it was the dashboard of Stella's Crown Vic only it wasn't rolling down a hill, it was right in front of me, rushing toward my face as she hit the brakes. Stella was against the steering wheel. I had a seat belt on, Doris didn't. The steamer trunk came between Doris and the dashboard. The car slowed down with a jolt.

I gasped. "Where are we?"

Stella's voice trembled a little. "We just got off the Jersey Turnpike and on to the Garden State Parkway."

"Does this car have airbags," I said.

"There's a driver side airbag. Not the passenger side." Stella looked a little pale. After we went through a toll plaza, the car picked up speed in what felt like a lunge. I was feeling pinned to the back of my seat. The speedometer needle was bouncing over 100. I was still groggy but wide awake.

"Hey Stella," I said. "Can you slow down?"

Stella looked over at me. "You fell asleep, Kay. I thought you wanted to talk to us?"

"I pulled an all-nighter last night. I couldn't stay awake. Sorry."

"That's too bad. Cause we just got done talking about the call center."

"When?"

"When you were asleep."

"Oh. What'd I miss?"

Stella threw back her hair. "Too late, Kay. We stopped for gas, you missed that, too."

"Seriously, what'd you say?"

"I don't think us girls wanna go into that again."

"Me neither," said Marge. "That was enough call center crap for one day."

I looked outside and couldn't tell where we were. It was starting to rain. Stella was changing lanes.

"Seriously, what'd you say?"

Doris moved her trunk around on her lap. Stella rapped a ring on her finger against the steering wheel like she was keeping time to a beat. Stella drove to the clock.

Doris hiccupped. "Stella, tell Kay the story about Arizona."

"Me tell a story? Why me?"

"You wanted to tell it this morning, Stell. You said 'I wanna tell this chick about my time in Arizona.' That chick is Kay."

"When'd I say that?"

"I didn't write down when you said it, but you said it."

"I didn't know I was signing my life away."

"You'll just tell a little story, Stell. Nobody's gonna know."

I almost got out my tape recorder but was afraid it would pick up the sound of the motor and the road, not Stella's voice. The Crown Vic sounded like it really *did* have 150,000 miles on it. I left it in my cargo pants.

Stella looked at me. "I wish you didn't go askin everybody about bein married."

"Why?"

"Because it's not something you get over right away. I'm leavin that out of my story."

"Who'd you get married to, Stella?"

Stella threw back her hair. "Forget the gettin married part. I'm not thinkin about my ex. I'm thinkin of this guy I met in a night club in PA."

Doris laughed her call center laugh. "You met him in the eighth grade, Stella. Don't act like you met some hot guy in a club just because Kay don't know it's bullshit and that there's no nightclubs in Altoona."

"There is, too!" Stella shouted. "There's Club Coconuts where we hung out, so there *is* a nightclub in

Altoona! You think you're so freakin smart, Doris? We *were* in the eighth grade but he went in the military later. I left my ex and followed him out to Nellis Air Force Base in Nevada. *Then* I found him in one of them legal cat houses they got outside Vegas. The only reason I went there was to get a T-shirt and I find him instead. He's *paying* to get it there instead of givin it to me at home. He's givin them *our* rent money, right? What the fuck! I took my kids and moved to Tucson. Arizona."

"Why'd you do that," I said.

The car swerved into the slow lane as Stella eased off the gas and pointed at me. "I'm not telling you the *why*, I'm just telling you the *what.*"

"Ok then, what?"

"I got a job in the payday loan industry."

Doris clucked. "The bitch that was bonin her old man set her up in it and sent her to AZ—right, Stella? Can't say she never done nothin for you, huh."

My pen skipped. "Wait...so you met this person who got you a job in the payday loan business and she worked in a brothel that your boyfriend...patronized?"

"That whole part of the story is somethin I'm leaving out, too. But Doris is right, I went to Tucson and got a job at a store front owned by a chain makin payday loans around 2008, before the state closed them down in Arizona. You can get them in Nevada and a bunch of other places. Payday loans are for usually a couple hundred dollars, you don't often see em for over $3000. They give you a loan, but you have to pay it back in two weeks—by payday. The borrower pays up but now they're broke again, so they get another loan. It's called flipping. I flipped a lotta lotta loans."

"This is what you did before you worked at the student loan call center?"

"I did student loans first, then payday, then back

to student loans. In payday I did loan origination but didn't see the debt collection side until right before I left Tucson. I was too busy figurin out how to live on what they paid me."

"How much did they pay you, Stella?"

"Not enough, *Kay*. So I got an auto title loan in Tucson. I drove up to a place on Broadway Boulevard with this gold rocket ship on the roof that said WE BUY GOLD. They're gold buyers, too, but more auto title. As soon as I walk in this guy grabs the car keys outa my hand. I said, 'Hey, where you goin?' He says he wanted to see how the car runs. Then he takes a picture of it while I had this vision of somebody driving off with it."

"Somebody who's not you," said Peg.

"Right. I got the keys back but first they made copies. They loaned me $500. I can't remember what I spent the money on, just that I needed it. The money was gone the next day. Easy come, easy go."

"But then you couldn't handle the auto title payments," Peg reminded.

Stella turned around. "Let me tell my own freakin story, ok?" She took a deep breath. "So I couldn't make the payments. And somebody drove off with the car."

"Who drove off with your car," I asked.

"The auto title lender. I missed *one* payment. One freakin payment and they take my car. I woke up one morning and there's an empty space where there used to be a car. There was tumble weed, but no car. I guess they came with a tow truck cause I got a bill from a towing company over this car I don't have."

"What kind of car?"

"A car with four wheels." Stella smacked her forehead. "Lord, I didn't plan that right. I was living near the old part of Tucson, the payday loan place is out at the other end of Speedway Boulevard. When I saw that empty space where there used to be a car it hit me: how do I get my kids to day care? The day care center is in still another part of town. Everything's spread out. You can't do this by bus in Tucson. There's almost no busses and they're slow."

I was writing this down. No one noticed. "So then what happened?"

"I stole a car."

"Gurrrl...." Peg hissed.

"How do you think I got back to PA?"

"Gurrrrrrrl!" Peg and Margot growled together. "Faster pussycat, kill, kill!"

Stella brightened a little. "It was my ex-new boy-friend from Tucson who done it. He got a car started for me, drove it by my place and parked it in the driveway but left it running with the door open. He called it his last act of love."

"Did he go down on you first?" asked Peg.

"Goddam it this is serious!" Stella shouted. "This was an act of love, believe me, knowing we'd never meet again. Hard-wiring a car ain't like back in the day. All the security features now? It's not really hard-wiring and takes a real pro. But he got it down. I drove back east in a Mercedes Benz, late model. I stayed off the toll roads where they got cameras. That took forever."

"How'd you get hired at the call center," I asked.

"They knew me from before. What they don't know don't hurt them. I parked it on the street outside Harrisburg and my sister picked us up. That part was good timing, that was perfect."

I leaned forward. "How long ago was this?"

"Too long. Don't worry about it. I turned that into an omen. It grew into an omen, as big as a diamond ring on your finger. The omen says go to Atlantic City.

Then it became a vision."

She had an omen. And a vision. I wanted to stay away from that so she wouldn't talk omens and visions all the way to Atlantic City. I didn't want to discuss her kids yet but if the choice was between her omens and her kids, give me the kids.

"You have kids, Stella," I said. "Is it hard making ends meet?"

"If I got an auto title loan, what do you think?"

"It'd be great if I could see some of your financial records. Maybe they tell a story. Really, Stella, I have kids and I'm single."

Stella didn't reply. No one was talking. I noticed the radio on the dashboard. I was afraid that if it got too quiet, somebody might turn it on.

"Did the payday loan business remind you of the student loan business," I asked.

Stella moved back to the fast lane. "I wondered about that. Sometimes it did when people ended up worse off than they started. With payday loans the interest usually starts at 300%, 400%. With student loans, the interest is way less but you're borrowing in the tens of thousands of dollars, not hundreds, so it can still act like a payday loan."

"I don't know if I agree that payday loans and student loans are that much alike," said Doris.

Stella shrugged. "So don't agree. It don't matter if it's a student loan or a payday loan, borrowers are still bitchin."

"I think student loans and payday loans can seem the same," said Peg, who had kind of a squeaky voice. "It's still predatory lending. How many times have you talked to a borrower who got a student loan of like $25,000, paid back $15,000 and ten years later they owe like $50,000? They're on the phone going *how can this happen to me?* It can go on for *decades*. That student loan is like a payday loan on crystal meth."

Marge blew smoke over my shoulder. "I don't know if I see it that way. With student loans at least you get school out of it. But if it's a crappy school or you don't know why you're there..."

"Maybe Stella's right, Peg," said Margot. "She got more experience in the lending side than us."

"What you hear all the time is the regret," Stella said. "People keep sayin they're *sorry* after it's too late. It don't matter if they blame the system and who knows what kind of a system this is we live under. I get bitches cryin on the phone sayin, oh, I went to law school or oh, I'm so smart, how can this be happenin to me? I don't care if you wanted to be a lawyer or a doctor or where you *thought* you'd end up, if you get a call from me, you're a proven loser. They all talk about how sorry they are, but it's not sorry because they can't pay, it's sorry that they borrowed, believe me."

Doris laughed. "And then the borrowers get mad like *you* did this to them."

"Right!" Stella exclaimed. "They get pissed when you can't tell them what they wanna hear—and then they take it out on me. They get in *my* freakin face like *their* problem is *my* fault. I had a law school prick on the phone threaten me because he borrowed $200,000 that he couldn't pay back to go to some shit law school. Is that, like, *my* fault? He said he was gonna wait for me outside the call center and crack my skull with a pool cue. I told my supervisor to call the cops and he wouldn't do it. Now if it was *him* gettin threatened, he'd get the state troopers on that loser prick."

The hum of the road was back. Stella started to laugh.

"And here's me, Stella Recker, who finished high

school by the skin of my teeth, telling somebody who went to law school that they were dumb about their student loans. I'm layin down the law to *them*. I wish I could see the look on their face. The bitches."

I stopped writing. I thought about what she said about borrower regret, which is like buyer's remorse in reverse. I passed the point of regret a long time ago with Leenie's loan. Things may still work out—sort of—and then I'll have fewer regrets. If nothing works out, I'll have more. The expectation when she left for grad school was that there'd be no regrets, none. I was going to say something about myself, then thought *stay out of this*.

"Seriously, Stella," I asked, "do you think there's a real difference between a payday loan, an auto title loan and a student loan?"

Stella gave me a suspicious look. "You ask too many questions, Kay. And you know what? I want to take some of my answers back."

"I don't know what you mean, Stella."

"What have you been writin there?"

"Just some notes."

"I wanna see what you wrote. You need to show me."

The car swerved as Stella reached across Doris and tried to grab the notebook. Doris put her hand on the wheel. "Stella—watch where you're going!"

"You can see it when we get to Atlantic City," I said.

"Stella!" Doris and Peg yelled, "Drive!"

"There's a semi right behind you!"

An air horn blew as we were veering off the road while a long semi-truck went by. Doris gasped, "Those motherfuckers!"

"Those cocksuckers aren't allowed on parkways!"

screamed Margot.

Stella wrestled with the wheel and for a moment couldn't control the car. She was panting when she cut into the slow lane and righted the Crown Vic. Horns were blaring behind us.

Stella pointed at me. "I'm not gonna say one more fuckin thing until I see what you're writin!"

"It was just some notes!" I shoved the notebook into my pants. The car started to veer across two lanes again on the four-lane road. I could feel everyone hold their breath. Doris put her hand on Stella's shoulder.

"Stell...take it easy...."

"Who said I'm not takin it easy!" Stella screamed.

"Why are you in this bad mood, darlin?"

"Who said I'm in a bad mood!"

Doris's voice sounded almost soothing. "Stell, you don't wanna take this out on Kay. She's tryin to look into something that's real shady or illegal. It's not about you or me, it's about something that's out of whack and bigger than us. Kay's right to check this out and write about it."

"And *you* started this by tipping her off about the call center, *Doris*."

"So what? I think Kay means well."

Stella leaned over the wheel. "Do you mean well, Kay?"

"Yes."

They had taken their Statue of Liberty visors off and were fanning their faces. The windows went up, the windows went down but the cigarette smoke drifted around. It was warm in the car. When the windows were up I thought I could hear them all breathing.

"Here's the kind of thing I think Kay's gettin at," Doris said. "There was a chick at the call center named Destiny Childs. That chick from West Philly? She came before me. Remember her, Stell?"

"Yup. She's back at a McDonald's somewheres."

"Fedloan was servicing her loan from a for-profit college that went delinquent after she got hired. One day she came in and had to call herself about her loan. The supervisor knew. It was a joke."

"Did she leave herself a message?" I asked.

"Of course. The people you call, their phone numbers, what they said if they answered, you report all that. It's on your screen."

"Then what?"

"I guess she had to call herself again. I don't really know. She wasn't at home because she was at Fedloan. She could have called her cell phone if she had one."

"Destiny was fun," Peg giggled. "Even on the job."

"She get in trouble?" I asked.

"She was already in trouble if you count the loan," Doris continued. "Even if you work for a servicer you still pay. If you don't, they send you to a collection agency. Your salary gets garnished. How all that works is above my pay grade."

Stella gnawed on her fingernails. "Your credit score gets killed and you can't borrow. If it's credit cards you can maybe make a deal with the lender. Federal student loans? No deal."

The needle was bouncing on the speedometer. I thought of the numbers on my credit score and remembered again that before Leenie's loans I rarely borrowed anything. My first husband, Ned, my son Rod's father, was a stickler for having no debt. Mortgages were an exception. And car loans. Credit cards, he said, were evil.

He dropped out of college like I did and got a job as an air traffic controller at Denver International

Airport. There was enough distance between the 1981 PATCO strike, when Ronald Reagan fired all the air traffic controllers, and when he got hired so that you couldn't say he was a scab. That job and being pregnant were among the reasons I married him. His mantra was, "This is a good job. It'll keep us out of debt."

But he took the job home. He not only took it home, he took it to bed. We'd be having sex and he'd hear airplanes. We'd be doing it with him on top of me, everything moving along nicely, he had a way of rubbing me with the head of his cock but not quite going in that was really nice. Then he'd go in. Then he'd stop. He'd pull out, roll over and say, "I almost crashed some planes today." He'd be very still. I'd lie there on my back, my hand around his half-hard hard-on and say, "It's ok, baby. Tomorrow is another day." He'd sit up and say, "Yeah, right! Tomorrow's another day when I might crash some planes!" Some nights he'd just lie awake, listening for planes that weren't there.

He was the wrong person for the job, good job or not. He wasn't a bad guy but was kind of an indifferent father. You don't find out about that until it's too late. I don't know, I felt sorry for him and he was cute; that's why I married him. My maternal instincts are often misplaced. And I was a kid.

Rod was in grade school when Ned had a nervous breakdown. I was never sure that his breakdown wasn't a trick to get rid of me and Rod. We *did* have no debt and made some money when we sold our idyllic suburban house. Ned left the state while my son and I moved to the crappy part of Denver for a while. I saved my share of the house sale. It was an amicable break-up to end all amicable break-ups. Actually, it wasn't that simple. I haven't seen him in a long time. I think I'm fine with leaving it that way. Sometimes I miss him.

"Anybody here owe money?" asked Peg. "Besides Kay, I mean."

Stella was irate. "You getting into my personal shit, too, Peg? Why is everybody out to get me?"

"You don't owe anything, then," Peg said quickly. "Fine, I'll put you down as a no."

"Don't put me down as nothing. I'm here for a reason. I was summoned here. It's not like a summons from a court. It came from inside of me, like my kids, but from something outside me, too. I don't want to say nothing more."

It got very quiet. "Why don't you want to say more," Peg asked.

"Because of you know why."

"Kay doesn't know," said Doris. "Why don't you tell her?"

"It's because of what I'm owed. And it's because Donald Trump owes me."

"Oh, Stella," Margot brayed. "When are you going to let that go?"

"I'm never gonna let that go. My sister owes me, too, but she's broke."

"What does your sister owe you?" I asked.

There was a long silence.

"What does Donald Trump owe you," I said.

Stella's voice dropped. "I sent an audition tape for that show, *The Apprentice*. I never heard back."

"You didn't go about it the right way," said Peg.

"You weren't that good," Doris whispered.

"I was, too! The show takes people in sales! I was in sales! I did telemarketing for that contractor, The Miracle One-Day Bathroom guys. They build you a bathroom in one day."

"How'd that work out," I said.

"Don't worry about it! I'm gonna still get what's

mine!" Stella bit her thumb. "I'm biding my time until the time is right. For real."

"How much is yours, Stell," Doris said. "Give me a thing or a number."

"I don't have to give you a *thing* or a *number!*"

"Then how do you think you're gonna get what you wanna get?"

"I'll send in another audition tape. I'll nail the audition, whatever."

"What if you don't?"

"I'll nail it in person. I'll knock on the door of *The Apprentice* until they let me in."

"Even if you get in," said Peg, "what if nothing happens?"

"I'll give up some pussy."

There was a pause some rustling in the back seat. I thought I could hear the tires on the road.

"What if *that* won't work?" said Peg.

The highway was whining.

"Well, if it don't work, then that's it," said Margot. "Alls she did was give up some pussy."

"Yeah, but what if she has to do it over and over again?" said Peg.

"What if she gives up pussy to people who can't pull no strings for her?" added Marge.

"Yeah, there's that," Margot added gravely. "You don't wanna be givin it to the wrong people. That's if anybody's interested. Just sayin, Stell."

Doris squirmed. Stella was seething. They were mocking her, probably not for the first time. Although not Doris. This was an opening for me to say something, something encouraging. But I couldn't encourage her in any of this. I wanted to tell her...what in the world could I tell her? Anything I said would be the wrong thing.

Stella took a deep breath. "The other thing is I'm going to Trump's casino. The odds are better there like Doris's father said." She exhaled. "I gotta break out of this bad streak I'm in. I'm in a vicious circle. The call center pays me every two weeks. So why am I always broke? I feel like somebody's always playin me. I'm due for a break. For real."

"What if you lose at Trump's" said Peg in a low voice.

"If the advice you're givin me is don't go, don't bother," Stella fumed. "I can think of a lotta lotta people who would say 'Stella—go for it.' I'm not sayin how much money I'm gonna win, because I don't wanna jinx this. Anybody got anything negative to say, keep it to yourself."

I ran through a list of remarks I could make, discarding them as I went. I could say, "I don't like negative people, either, Stella. See? We have something in common." But if she said, 'All I've heard out of you, Kay, is a bunch of negativity' I'd have to defend myself. I'd be back where we started. I didn't even know where that was.

I watched the signs go by as if I was going to find the advice I was looking for there. Every casino billboard, from the Sands to Caesar's were splashed with concert photos of The Eagles, Bobby Rydell, Jefferson Starship, Chaka Kahn and a thousand Elvis impersonators above a tiny tag line at the bottom: *Gambling Problem? Call 1-800-Gambler.* Would anybody answer the phones?

Peg started to hum a song. I felt an outburst coming. A smart remark would come from the backseat, then another and Stella would explode. The shimmy in the front end was back, but this time there was a rhythmic rattle, like one pipe hitting another. More miles went by. There was no outburst, no tirade. I thought someone was bound to say a discouraging word about *something*, but there was silence. Peg stopped humming. When she stopped, the rattle coming from underneath the car died down. Signs went by. The rattle started again. I was tired. The rattle was keeping me awake. I was hungry. I had visions of pizza boxes outside the conference room where I spent the night.

Exit 100 was fading into Stella's rearview mirror. I shouldn't have asked her for financial documents, not yet. That's often tricky and it doesn't always help. People usually don't know what they have. Getting somebody's records can be as bad as not having any at all. They dump their bank statements and cancelled checks on you and expect you to tell them what it all means while they leave things out. Then after you've looked at everything, you find that it doesn't help you tell their story—or that it contradicts their story. Stella gave every indication that she was broke herself. She could say more, then take everything back if she didn't like the way it sounded.

When we got where we were going I'd have to mend some fences. I was worried that I'd already lost Stella. After she lost her money, her mood could go from bad to baleful. I could try Peg, Margot or Marge. Marge seemed the least talkative. There was no good way to plan this. Stella was pushing the needle over 90.

"Stella...could you slow down a little," I said. The speedometer flirted with 85.

"It's awful quiet back there," said Doris."

Margot's hoop earrings jangled. "What do you want me to do, Doris, sing you a song?"

Peg clapped her hands. "Oh, cool! Let's sing a

song!"

Nobody sang. Nobody said anything for a while. Stella eased off the gas. "What are we, Campfire Girls."

Peg was giddy. "Who cares! Just as long as we sing. It's too quiet in here. Stella's too cheap to get her radio fixed."

Stella punched the buttons on the radio. Nothing happened.

"Ok," Doris sighed, "what should we sing?"

"No Jesus songs," warned Margot. "That's where I draw the line."

"What's wrong with Jesus songs?" said Marge.

"It's not that kind of trip."

"The trip doesn't matter," said Peg. "The songs don't have to match the trip."

"How about 'The Old Rugged Cross,'" said Doris. "Remember that one?"

"Church music," Marge raved. "Let's all praise Jesus."

"I remember that song," said Peg. "The melody, just not the words."

"I can just hear the lyrics," said Margot. "I'm not sure about the melody."

Peg began to hum. "You start it, Doris."

Doris started to sing.

On a hill faraway, stood an old rugged cross
The emblem of suffering and shame
And I love that old cross
Where the dearest and best
For a world of lost sinners was slain...

She stopped. Her voice had mutated again. It was different from her laugh, different from her call center voice or her conversational voice. Different from the way she sounded in person. That warbly voice became deep, like she had been a trained contralto. At the end she hit a high note on *sinners*.

"That's beautiful, Doris." Peg exclaimed.

"I didn't know you could do that," said Marge.

"Sure you did," said Doris. "I sang that at the old Methodist Church. You were there."

"You should be singin, somewhere Doris," said Peg. "You should be in a show."

"Keep goin, Doris," said Marge.

So I'll cherish the old rugged cross
Till my trophies at last are laid down
And I'll cling to the old rugged cross
And exchange it someday for a...for a...for a...

Doris held the last note, then stopped.

Stella leaned forward. "You'll exchange it for a *what?*"

Doris seemed stumped. "I forget the rest of the song. I can't remember what comes next."

"Oh I love that part," wailed Peg.

"I think there's more verses," Doris said.

Margot flipped a butt out the window. "Are you sure you got the words right? What in the world would you exchange the old rugged cross for? A Walmart gift card?"

"You don't exchange the old rugged cross for nothing!" shouted Marge. "Not silver or gold, that would be sacrilegious and heathenism!"

"We could start it from the beginning," suggested Peg. "Maybe that will help us remember the last line."

Nobody sang. I watched the mile markers and the speedometer. Nobody sang for a mile, then another, then another. I was trying to count them. Not every mile had a marker. We were making time, regardless of what time it was. For some reason I was elated.

Then I wondered what the chances were that we'd get to Atlantic City without singing any more songs. If they could sing one song, what's stopping them from singing another. The tires sang to the road.

"How about we sing 'Shut Up and Drive,'" said Margot. "By Rihanna. From 2007. We did that song before. A lot."

"Yeah, we know that one," said Doris.

"Too old," said Peg.

Doris turned around. "'The Old Rugged Cross' is like *really* old."

"There's old and there's *old*," said Stella. "That's a different kind of old. So sing me a line from that song."

"I'm looking for a driver who's qualified, *Stella*," sang Margot.

"You think that you're the one, Stell?" Marge deadpanned. "Step into my ride—you skank."

Peg started to sing from the back seat into my ear while I girded myself. Margot mimicked the song's guitar hook. Then the handclaps, then the lyrics. I thought I could tune this out without putting my hands over my ears.

That didn't work. After a few minutes of this my head was ready to explode. All five of them were belting out this song that I remembered hearing on the street, on my computer or out of a boom box, although this was probably after boom boxes.

The windows were vibrating. So were my ear drums. I opened my window. The vibrating didn't stop with my ear drums. I felt it in my chest. They knew every word, then riffed on the chorus and made up their own words. Their version of what was probably a four-minute song went on for ten minutes, it came in waves.

My eyes were on the road, Stella's hands were on the wheel, she was singing and I wasn't. My eyes started to water. The verses cascaded on top of each other like the car was an echo chamber.

They were shouting each other down—shut up and drive shut up and drive shut up and drive until the words were unintelligible. The song collapsed and faded out like it would at the end of a record. The singing died out over and over and over. I closed my window. I was stunned by the noise.

Outside I could hear the wind. It was raining. After they stopped, it was like the sound could have continued at the decibel level of a dog whistle.

An earlier silence returned. I wanted Stella to drive faster again. I wanted to get there.

Stella leaned over the wheel. "How come you weren't singin, Kay?"

"I can't sing."

"Why not?"

"Really, you don't want to hear me sing."

Doris seemed genuinely offended. "You're not gonna sing on our girly road trip? What kind of crap is that?"

"You *don't* want to hear me sing."

Margo blew smoke from the back. "You oughta be singin, Kay."

"Sing for your supper, Kay," Stella said.

"Why don't you just drive, Stella."

"It's sing or get out and walk," said Marge.

"Yeah," said Stella. "Sing or get out and walk."

Some more mile markers went by, more signage pointing out rest stops with which restaurants and what gas stations. The car slowed down. The sign for Exit 74 of the Garden State Parkway went by. Another said Forked River. Where or what was Forked River?

Stella moved into the fast lane. We were driving into a rain squall that was coming from the left, the side of the car that faced the ocean. The car swerved as Stella turned on the wipers. The wheels went off the asphalt as we drove onto a median, a slice of forest that grew between the north and southbound lanes. The car felt like it had no shock absorbers. The ground became bumpy followed by a crunching sound like we went over a thousand of beer bottles. Something was breaking underneath the tires. I waited for it to get louder. Then it stopped. The car was 100 feet from the highway. Stella put it in park and turned off the motor. She looked straight ahead.

"Are you gonna sing, Kay?"

"No."

"It's sing or get out and walk."

It became quiet. They seemed to be waiting. I glanced at Margot in the back seat. She butted out her cigarette and rustled with a map. "There's only about 20 miles to go," she declared. "You might get most of the way there before it got dark if you start walking now."

"If we throw her out how's she gonna write her story?" Doris asked.

"Fuck her and fuck her story," said Stella.

My ears were ringing. I was on another highway, years ago, with Leenie's father, my second husband, who was threatening to throw me out of the car south of Cape Girardeau, MO. He was serious. He relented because it was getting dark. I remembered the fight we had, but not what it was about. Leenie and Rod were scared because I said if I left, I was taking them with me. I'll bet they saw themselves out on the road. I wasn't sure they would go with me or what I really would have done. I talked to them about it later. I talked to them for a long time. We talked and talked. That was a long time ago. I can't remember everything we said.

It was raining hard. I wondered how long it would be before it got dark. Margot's hoop earrings jangled.

"You could still stay," Stella offered. "But only if you sing."

"Gotta sing for it, Kay."

"What song am I singing?"

"Pick your favorite."

I hesitated. "I'm not singing."

We sat. I don't know how long we sat for. Stella was rapping her ring finger on the steering wheel. "Are we kidding?" said Peg.

"I think we're serious," said Marge from the back.

I could hear the traffic go past, the rain water washing over car tires. I thought I heard birds. The wind. I wondered what it would be like to stand out in the wind. If we had been on the road, we would have covered some of the 20 miles Margot said we had left.

Doris's trunk poked me in the ribs. I looked at Doris. "What have you got in your trunk?"

"My trunk? What do you care?"

"You got your apartment keys in there? Your wallet?"

"Yeah. So?"

"Maybe Doris and Kay could have a sleep over," laughed Margot. "A pajama party."

I opened the door, wishing I hadn't worn heels, and put one foot on the ground then both hands on the handle of Doris's trunk. The rain was coming down sideways and the wipers weren't keeping the water off the windshield. I yanked the trunk away from her and put it outside the car. "If I'm leaving, Doris, I'm taking your trunk with me."

Doris looked surprised. She didn't move. "Hey—what do you want my trunk for?"

"I might take it on a trip."

"What are you talkin about?"

"I could throw it in the middle of the Garden State Parkway, too. Or I could put it through Stella's windshield. You got a preference?"

Stella leaned over the steering wheel. "What did you say?"

I slid a little more out of the car. "Stella, you want to get out of the way before the trunk goes through the windshield?"

Stella gazed half at me, half out the windshield while the wipers splashed water on it. Then she sat up. "Yeah, I know who you are, Kay. You're just somebody else out to fuck with me."

"Maybe you're better off with no windshield since the wipers don't keep the water off."

Peg reached across the seat and touched my shoulder. "Kay...don't."

Stella pointed at me. "Kay, if I had to, I could talk you out of doing this."

"Start talking, then."

"You wanna see me talk? I'm the biggest talker you ever seen."

"Stella, let's skip this," said Peg. "Let Kay give Doris her trunk back. Then let's get going."

"I think I agree with Peg," said Margot.

Marge was silent. Stella was incredulous. "So Peg and Margot are lining up with Kay? This bitch comes here like some brainiac, like she's all that and tellin people when they can smoke—and you're on *her* side?"

"That's not what I came for," I said."

"You think you're messing with us?" said Stella.

"That's not what I'm here for."

Let me tell you something about Doris, Kay. You think you know her but you really don't."

Doris held her arms out, one in front of Stella, the other touching me. "Hey—Stella. It feels like we're not getting what we came here for, right Stell?"

"I didn't come on this trip to hang out with this cunt Kay!"

"We didn't come to fight with Kay, either right? Anybody here don't agree with that?"

Peg squeezed Stella's shoulder. "I think we're only kidding."

"What if I'm serious?" said Stella. She turned around. "Are you serious, Marge?"

"I don't know. What am I serious about?"

The rain was getting serious. Doris seemed stuck, she couldn't move. I imagined the six of us standing around this car with a broken windshield. Even if they put Humpty together again I could still be walking down the road in high heels. I'd be getting soaked. I was already getting wet just sitting here.

"Stella," Peg said. "Stop this. Just shut up and drive."

For a moment I thought Stella was going to tell us all to get out and walk. Then I thought she was just going to sit and not move until she figured out what to do. We waited.

There seemed to be factions forming. Peg, Marge and Margot, were squished together in the back—I thought they just wanted to get going. Doris didn't seem to be in a faction yet. She probably didn't have a neighbor in her building with a spare set of apartment keys and she wanted her trunk. Stella was digging in her heels, but wanted her windshield. Even if the trunk wouldn't break it, there'd still be a crack.

Doris wasn't going to get her trunk until I was sure we were getting back on the road. I still had one foot out the door. I was wet but for now I didn't care. They were stirring in the back seat, murmuring.

Doris nudged me. "Are we good, Kay?"

"What are we good for, Doris?"

"Let's put our differences to one side. We're good to go, right?"

"Hey! I'm drivin and I get the say—"

"Stella! Shut up and drive!"

Stella didn't answer. She didn't turn on the ignition right away. A silent countdown began leading up to when she would start the car. I noticed how wet the ground was.

She started it. I gave Doris her trunk. I got a funny look back from her, like she wasn't that upset. The engine stalled. Stella tried again and it stalled again. The rain was stopping. The clouds were moving fast but the car went nowhere. It seemed like the car wouldn't start, once and for all, when she coaxed it to life. Marge shouted, "We're born again!" Margo muttered *shut up.* I wondered if the Crown Vic would get them back to Pennsylvania when it came time to go, windshield or no windshield.

I was back in and closed the door. The trunk was back on Doris's lap. I braced myself, in case Marge grabbed me by the throat or Stella reached across Doris and punched me. I thought of a song I used to sing to my kids. If I had just sung a few bars of *The Wheels of The Bus Go Round and Round* would we have avoided this? I'm stubborn. I often pick the wrong time to be stubborn. I think I'm getting my way, I think I'm getting what I want and when I stop and look around I don't have what I thought I was going to get at all.

I just wanted to get out of this place. Except for

Stella and maybe Marge, the call center posse didn't want to stop. The wheels of the Crown Vic were slipping.

Stella rocked it back and forth, shifting from drive to reverse to summon that extra *umph*. She summoned it. It wasn't there. She threw it into park and wiped the hair from her face. "We're gonna have to get out and push."

I rubbed my eyes. "What happened?"

"We're stuck. Everything is wet. The tires are slipping. It's all grass and weeds."

"How could we be stuck in grass?"

"Stella's freakin tires are *bald*," Margot jeered. "That's how."

Stella unbuckled her seat belt. "It's not the tires. One rear wheel is in a rut, I can feel it. Peg has to drive. Everybody else, get out and push."

No one moved. The skies opened up. They looked out the windows.

"I don't want my clothes to get soaked," Margot whined.

"It's either get soaked or stay stuck."

"Couldn't we wait until it stops," Marge moaned.

We waited. I looked at my watch. It wasn't there, I didn't bring it. I thought of the trip I used to take from Denver to Lincoln, Nebraska and back, twice a month. Getting to the Nebraska border was almost a third of the trip, and by the time you got to the eastern end of the state you've been driving for about eight hours. You drive into central standard time on the way out and gain an hour but lose it on the way back. Ned, my first husband, was from there and his mother lived in Lincoln.

That's what those trips were about. My parents were dead, his father was dead, she was the only grandparent. The weekend would disappear along the highway, like we left it there and drove away. Rod was ok on the way out but by the time we left Lincoln for Denver he was fit to be tied. Route 80 was a straight line and flat, but in the winter semis jack-knifed and the whiteouts could obscure anything beyond the windshield. We argued about going through Kansas. My ex said it was faster, I said it wasn't. The car always seemed packed, not like Stella's car, but in a different way even if it was only me, Rod and his father.

Rod was sick on those trips. He was sick a lot. I worried that he had a chronic disease. It was me, my son, his father and my son's potentially chronic disease. We didn't know what it was, the pediatricians we had made me crazy with their indecisiveness. I was afraid he wouldn't live to see high school. Come to think of it, he cried on the way out to see grandma *and* on the way back. When he wouldn't stop crying I sang to him. I sang and sang in the hope that he would stop.

His father refused to sing. Ned changed diapers, I'll give him that, but the sonuvabitch wouldn't sing a note. I can't sing and I did all the singing. The singing I did wasn't singing. It was a flat, recitation of the words to Rod's one and only favorite song.

> *The wheels of the bus go round and round*
> *Round and round, round and round*
> *The wheels of the bus go round and round*
> *All over town*

Mile after mile. Day after day. Year after year. There were times when I wanted to cry. There were times when I did. There was one time, when there was snow on both sides of the road that blew into a white-out that stretched into the horizon, when Rod stopped crying and watched me cry instead.

Those trips to Nebraska brought out the worst in us. We argued about whether Rod should have his tonsils out. Infected tonsils, his father said, are what's making him sick and they have to come out. That's not done anymore, I argued. It's absolutely done, his father argued back.

After Ned's mother died and the trips ended, Rod kept his tonsils and stopped getting sick.

We split up. It was like...I don't know what it was like. It was like we were staying together to avoid having to tell my mother-in-law thing were going sideways. We had to tell Rod, which was much worse. But he stopped getting sick after we broke up. It was like magic. There were times when I wanted to call Ned and say, "Hey, after we split up, Rod stopped getting sick. That's really something, huh?" I think I did call and tell him.

The rain stopped. Stella opened her door. After Doris warned her not to turn the ignition off, five of us went to the back of the car while Peg got behind the wheel. After a while they were standing there, not doing anything. I wanted to start pushing. They were acting like we'd just pulled up to the beach.

Stella was at the back, kicking the tires. "We're gonna have to lift the car."

"That's stupid," said Marge. "If the back wheels are off the ground you're not gonna move. We have to just push."

Doris went into the trees and came back with boards that she wanted to shove under the wheels to give them traction. Stella and Doris argued after they wouldn't fit. The idea was to drive over them.

The sun was lower in the sky. The sun was moving faster than this car. We'd push, take a break, push, take a break. We were almost knee-deep in slimy grass and vegetation that stuck to your clothes. It started to rain again. I didn't expect to find a jungle on a storm-swept day near a densely-populated part of the country that was also in the middle of nowhere. Stella tried to get us to push together. Then Doris tried. Then me. My shoes made me wobble. We all pushed. We all stopped, all at once when it began teeming again.

"I'm gonna go inside until the rain stops," said Margot. "I just bought this outfit. Why didn't we get a weather report before we left?"

"Why didn't Stella just stay on the freakin road?" Doris hollered. "What were you thinkin, Stell?"

We got back in the car. Peg was still behind the wheel. Stella was in the back. They were seething, muttering. Margot was in the middle and Marge kept nudging Margot, saying move over, move over. Stella started shouting.

"It wasn't my idea to take Kay with us on this trip! This was supposed to be *our* trip, not hers. God *damn* you, *Doris!*"

I remembered that I left my watch at work every time I looked at my wrist. The idea that I wouldn't get back tonight was something new, like the fuzzy dice hanging from Stella's rearview mirror that I just noticed. I thought of the conference room on the 23rd floor, then my desk on the 22nd floor. I imagined people coming back from lunch, standing next to my chair saying, "Have you seen Kay?" I was expecting a call from Euroclear on Monday. Bank Paribas and Northern Trust were calling. The rarified air of custodian banks competed with the smell of Stella's car, where cigarette smoke mixed with the faint odor of Naugahyde, a little like the smell of every car I'd ever owned.

Once I was driving with Leenie in her father's Pontiac and she said, "My brother Rod told me that the upholstery in our car is made of Naugahyde and that it doesn't come from a dead animal that you have to kill to get its skin, but from an animal called a Nauga. The Nauga walks on three legs and looks like a goat with a horn in the middle of its head. The Nauga sheds its skin every Friday and you just pick it up off the ground and turn it into seat covers so you don't have to kill it. Is that true, Mom?"

I'd just had an argument with her father and I was fretting about that. I snapped at her and said, "No, your brother played a trick on you, there's no such thing as a Nauga with skin that gets turned into seat covers!" The next thing I know she was crying. I tried to remember how I got out of that one. I was getting more and more tense. When I got tense, I had flashbacks to Leenie's childhood.

Doris nudged me. "Rain stopped. Time to get out and push."

There were scattered rain drops. The sky was no longer blue, it was turning pink and gray. We were pushing all at once. When we started, it was like we started on cue. We stopped when somebody gave up.

I still couldn't tell what was underneath the car or what kept it from moving but one moment we were stuck, the next moment the front wheels were on asphalt. Just like that, the car lurched forward. Traffic was just beyond the front bumper. Horns blared. Peg got out and Stella got behind the wheel. I stopped thinking about my desk. We were back inside. Marge and Margot lit up. The windows came down for a while.

Stella had to wait a long time to move into traffic. She gunned the engine when it started to die, then fish-tailed on the wet road. I could feel the posse exhale.

"Just so you know, we got off easy there," said Stella. "I thought we were gonna be there all night."

Margot coughed. "Shut up and drive, Stell."

"Me shut up? I bring you good news and that's all you can say?"

That front-end shimmy was back. Another silence returned, the sound of people packed into this car who might be on a different trip now. I had an inkling that they weren't really sure where they were going.

There could be a Plan B. Doris could say, "Let's do something else instead of gamble." *Plan ahead* wasn't their motto. I saw them in high school, wandering the halls together, then the corridors at Fedloan. I hadn't asked that question: where did you all meet each other? That might be where the story begins. If the answer was complicated, I wanted to get it all down, something I couldn't do with Doris's trunk slipping into my lap.

"Doris, move your trunk."

She gave me a little smile as she moved it. We went by the Barnegat exit, where you couldn't see Barnegat from the road. It seemed like we were moving away from the water.

Peg was humming. Not like she would burst into song, but she was humming. "I think that Rihanna song copied from some old surfer dudes," she said. "The Beach Boys. My dad used to play that record all the time."

"What record?" asked Doris.

"I can't remember the name but I remember the melody."

"Didn't know that," said Doris.

"That's what I think."

"Who'd the Beach Boys copy from?"

"Chuck Berry," said Peg.

"Who's Chuck Berry?"

I watched the speedometer. Stella was driving at exactly the speed limit. The needle didn't move, unless it was now broken like the radio. There was a different hum coming from inside the car than before.

"I think the words to that Beach Boys song are coming back to me," said Peg.

"As long as you don't sing it," I said.

"What if that's part of *the story*," Stella jeered.

"Yeah," said Margot, "you wanted *the story*."

"I'll leave that part out," I said.

Stella leaned over the wheel. "Do we get a say on what gets left in the story and what gets left out? Cause I got some ideas."

Margot laughed. "When did *you* ever get a good idea."

"I got good ideas!" Stella yelled.

Margot laughed. "Name one."

"Let's all sit down and talk later," I said. "Then we can hear everyone's ideas."

I don't think anyone heard me. I felt Stella's hands on the wheel. It was as though they all gripped the wheel together.

"Instead of an idea, here's a question," said Peg. "Who here thought about getting a job in a 911 call center?"

"Not me," said Margot. "I don't want the stress. Or the background check. I don't know nothing about it and neither do you."

"Yeah," said Doris. "Suppose it's somebody you know that calls? Suppose it's their sister with a drug over-dose. Or their brother."

Stella mumbled, "I heard you get a lie detector."

"What could you lie about in a 911 call center?" I said.

"That your friend wasn't hooked on pills and

didn't OD."

"You can't give up information that comes in on a 911 call," Marge insisted. "They make you sign all kinds of papers. You're locked down."

"How do you know that," said Margot.

"Because I know shit. That's how I know."

"Prescription meds," said Peg. "Ones you buy on the street. That's already the next big thing. I bet every other call's somebody that OD'd."

"There's certifications you need," said Marge. "You're dispatching state troopers. It's life and death. And even though you work with the state police I don't think it's a civil service job. I don't think you get the benefits."

I was trying to take the temperature inside the car. Everything was wet. Stella eyes were on the road. Margot, Peg and Marge couldn't sit still in the back seat. Doris was calm. I wondered how close I came to being left on the highway. Even if I cracked the windshield Stella could still drive the car.

I'd crossed a line. I didn't know where it was, but I think I'd crossed it. If I wasn't on the side that made me one of them, I wasn't a smart-ass bitch anymore, or not the same kind. They could say, "Ok, we put Kay in her place for a while—let it go." They weren't letting it go, though, I could tell. Each one of them probably had a different idea about that. Doris brought me on this trip at the last minute. They all could have said, "Don't bring Kay." Doris brought me anyway.

My clothes were puffy and sagged from the rain. When we were stuck I got a look at the posse and what they were wearing. It was the same outfit—hoodies. They were all different—and all wet—but still hoodies. I don't know if it was a fashion statement or something more—or less. People went shopping and this is what they found. Once you pulled that hood over your head you could disappear. Not totally, but sometimes just enough.

You could almost buy a hoodie for the price of dinner for two at Taco Bell. Billionaires wore hoodies. Mark Zuckerberg wore a hoodie. Jay Z wore a hoodie. People on the A train wore hoodies and my daughter wore a hoodie, even in Southern California. When was Obama going to wear a hoodie? Did Dick Cheney wear a hoodie when he went duck hunting?

Marge, who I got a good look at for the first time, had a desert camo hoodie. Margot had a black, designer-looking hoodie that complemented her hoop earrings, not an off-the-rack garment. Peg was small—probably why Stella had her get behind the wheel when we were stuck—and wore a pink hoodie that said *Pretty in Pink*. Stella had a jean jacket hoodie that matched her blue lipstick and eye shadow which ran down her face in the rain. The eye shadow made her look sad. Doris wore a plain gray hoodie that was invisible. Everyone's hair was wet. I wondered if they did a special mall run to dress for this trip. It used to be jeans. Now it was hoodies.

Peg leaned over the seat. "Stella, I think you gotta say you're sorry."

Stella turned to look at her. "Me say I'm sorry? For what?"

"Tell Kay you're sorry. Apologize."

"What do I gotta apologize for?"

"For being that way with her. We shouldn't have done that."

"It wasn't just me! Marge started it!"

"It's ok," I said. "Nobody has to apologize. We'll start over fresh. I'll buy everybody a drink when we get to the casino. Then we can talk."

There were no takers, not yet. If I could just get everybody together, exploit the cheesy expedient of springing for some booze—one round—maybe that would create the right atmosphere. These weren't people who'd say no to a free drink and it didn't matter who was buying. But I'd never been to a casino before. I didn't know if there'd be a quiet place where you could talk. Sitting at a noisy bar would be a waste. Where we did this would be moot if they held back.

We left the Parkway for a winding off-ramp to another highway. For a while we had been driving along the shore, then we were going toward the water. I didn't think I'd fall asleep, then I jerked forward with a start, so I must have dropped off. I imagined walking down whatever highway this was. When I left to meet them something told me not to wear high heels. I didn't listen to that something.

Traffic was backed up when we turned on to the Atlantic City Expressway, which divided in two at the start of a long stretch of deserted asphalt that ran down the middle.

Doris pointed at it. "What is this? A parking lot?"

"It's for the people that work in the casinos," Peg said. "They park here and take a bus. It's like going to the call center back in PA, right? You pay for parking then take a bus to the blue Fedloan building. You forgot?"

Stella looked at Doris. "She don't work there anymore. Out of sight, out of mind, huh Doris?"

We went over a bridge. It was twilight. There was water, the ocean, just beyond the blue horizon that was swirling into gray. About ten minutes later we drove by a bunch of outlet stores—Tanger, American Eagle, Aeropostale—before we were in what looked like a city.

Casinos filled the windshield.

Doris was pointing. "Here's a casino garage, Stell, pull in here."

"I wanna park on the street."

"I don't think you do."

"I don't wanna spend for parking."

"I think you better."

"If I want your advice, Doris, I'll ask for it."

"It'll be easy and no one will break into your car."

"If I'm paying for parking, I'm parking in Trump because that's where I'm playing—period!"

The wheels screeched as she turned left, left, and left again. The flow of traffic was confusing and pushed her toward the curb. The last left put her into a parking garage. We came to a stop.

"Goddam it, we're in freakin Caesar's when we gotta be in Trump!"

"It's just a parking garage," said Peg soothingly.

"The Caesar's garage fucks up my mojo!"

"Stell," they all said at once, "we'll run down to the street then go to Trump's! You won't know the difference!"

Cars pulled in behind the Crown Vic. Drivers leaned on their horns. It was too late to back out. Stella got out of the car, got in and slammed the door.

"You see what you did, Doris? You always do this to me!"

"I will make it up to you, darlin," Doris said calmly. "We'll make everything right."

We drove up to the next level. I thought of Doris putting on makeup as I put on my best smile, which no one was looking at. "So," I said, "can we all sit down and talk later."

The car swerved as Stella screamed. "Christ, Kay, is this about that fuckin story again? We're here to hit the casino, I mean right now!"

"I mean later, not right away."

Stella drove up another level and parked beside a concrete pillar. Gas, tolls and parking, everybody pays up. I dropped $20 into Stella's hand. Part of my lunch money for next week became her gas money. The posse started to pile out.

They were kind of standing around waiting for Stella. Her face was ashen when she got out of the car. I lingered for a moment.

The posse went down the ramps we drove up, I followed. I turned and saw Stella, a ways behind me. She seemed unsteady and walked in the shadows.

The others were waiting as I crossed the street. There was no Stella. We turned and waited until she emerged from the garage. Was she making her entrance or her exit?

For a minute I thought she was just going to faint. It was like she had come to this place where she told people she'd be made whole but was going to pieces once she understood that nothing good was about to happen.

She couldn't get back in her car and drive away. It was like the only option was to drive off a cliff, like Thelma without her Louise from that movie I almost saw where the two heroines drive their car into a canyon. The posse stared at her like she was getting ready to jump off a building.

Stella was sobbing. I wanted her to stop. What would she say if I gave her a hug? I wouldn't, but what would she say?

Peg went to her, like she was going to talk her off the edge. "Stella...tell me what's wrong."

"I'm angry, Peg. And I'm so afraid."

"Of what?"

"I'm so afraid. I'm falling. Somebody catch me before I fall."

Marge and Margot edged away. Doris seemed stuck. When Stella started to swoon, Doris ran to her and put her arm around her waist as she and Peg held her up.

Stella was taking baby steps. They were standing in the middle of the street. "I want one person to say that they love me," Stella gasped. "I feel so unloved."

A car honked and swerved around them. The driver yelled.

Peg went on tip toes and said, "I love you, Stelly," and kissed her on the cheek. After Peg left her embrace, Doris squeezed Stella's neck and kissed her. "I love you, Stella Wella! I want the world to know!"

A truck drove up behind me. I put my hands in my pockets as I got out of the way. My pen and my tape recorder were there, but my notebook wasn't. I tried to remember what was in it as I walked back into the parking garage. I'd written a passage about Stella's life in payday lending, one I could build on when I got back.

I found the Crown Vic and peered in the window. The notebook was lying on the seat but the door was locked. I remembered more of what Stella said and had nothing to write with. This was going to screw me up if I kept thinking about it and couldn't write it down. I couldn't let this go. I had to write *something*. I wrote Stella's license plate number on my arm.

The posse was on a ramp to the Boardwalk, huddled around Stella as they went. I followed. At the top of the ramp the posse turned right. I heard someone behind me. Doris grabbed my hand.

"Kay—let's take a walk."

"What?"

"Let's take a walk on the Boardwalk. We'll pass

Go and collect...how much do you get when you pass Go?"

"Won't they wonder where you are?"

"They won't notice for a while."

"When do I get to talk to them? By the way—"

"Now's not the time, Kay, and I'm sorry about what happened in the car. Stella got carried away."

"You wanna tell me about it?"

"Let's wait."

"Goddam you, Doris—"

"Me? What about you? You threatened to throw my trunk out in the traffic! With my keys and my wallet!"

"Doris—"

"Kay, I'm sorry! Ok?" She threw her arm around me. There was a caress as it fell from my shoulder. "Just gimme a chance to prove it. Really, it'll be ok. Think if it was all guys on this trip. Somebody woulda got their jaw broke by now."

"Is Stella in debt?"

"Take that up with her."

"What about your co-worker, Destiny Childs, who had a delinquent student loan. Is Stella in the same jam?"

Doris waved her hand. "Ask her."

"Can't you give me a hint?"

Doris waved her hand again. We seemed to be walking north, away from the Trump Hotel and Casino and toward the ocean side of the Boardwalk. I tried to be calm.

Small motorized carriages cruised the Boardwalk with people who seemed to have no destination. The summer was over. There were no life guards on the beach. Doris moved a few steps away, then moved close. When I looked at her I saw her trunk sticking out of Stella's windshield. Or out of her head.

The ocean was loud, crashing on the shore like in the movies. When we leaned on the railing, I noticed that the view was blocked by a huge pile of sand with a rag weed jungle on top like icing on a layer cake.

"Doris, what is this pile of dirt I'm seeing?"

"It's sand on top of a sand dune. It's a berm."

"Why did they dump this on the beach? You can't see the ocean."

"It stops the waves in case of a storm. They're called nor-easters. The water can flood over the Boardwalk."

I was feeling a chill. The wet clothes made me shiver. Doris moved closer to me as we walked away.

"So, Doris—"

"Like I said, I'm sorry things got out of hand. Stella didn't want you to come. I had to push some buttons to make that work."

"What buttons?"

"A lotta lotta buttons. I wasn't gonna leave you stuck in the weeds and the beer bottles."

"And you were going to do that how?"

"With a plan I didn't need. Really, didja have to walk to Atlantic City? You're here, right? Stella told you a true story about Arizona she didn't wanna tell. What more do you want?"

"I need more about the call center. I'd like to go there and get a look inside."

Doris gave me a funny look. "Stella didn't tell the real reason why she came here, ok? It's not just the gambling."

"How much will she spend?"

$300, maybe $400 on slot machines."

"So you'd need what, 1600 quarters? How long will it take to put them into a slot machine?"

"Depends. Stella's got her lucky slot machine at Trump's and if somebody's using it and she's gotta wait her turn, she won't even get started for a while."

"She thinks this will change her life?"

Doris waved her hand. "Another reason we're here is because of Stella's mother. She lives inland, not on the water, where she's gettin evicted from a housing complex. Stella and her don't get along, but Stell's upset and thinks she has to do *something*, she just don't know what. You can hate your mom, but you don't wanna see her evicted, right? It's pushing more buttons."

We moved to the next berm. A fog crept over the Boardwalk. I didn't want to get into Stella's mother yet. It seemed like I was on Doris's good side since we parked the car.

"Doris, even though you were hounding me with calls and making me late for work—and couldn't explain why my payments weren't being applied to the PLUS Loans—I wouldn't want Stella's mother to be evicted. If anything, it makes Stella seem human."

"Now that's weird, Kay. What's that supposed to mean?"

I felt a wave of vertigo. "I'm not sure."

Doris sneered. "And you're a writer?"

"I'm talking, not writing."

"Well, irregardless of what you think, Stella's embarrassed. She's somebody who believes in saving face. You don't wanna put her in a position where she can't save face."

"Like I said, if she told me her mother was being evicted, I'd feel bad."

"You're a stranger. And you called her a bitch."

"I'm not trying to embarrass her, Doris."

"Different people get shamed by different things.

Do you tell people you're in trouble because of your student loans?"

"Actually, it's my daughter."

"Actually, it's you—you co-signed the PLUS loans. And you don't tell anybody, do you?"

"Not normally."

"And it's because you don't want people to think you did something dumb, right?"

"I'd have to think about that."

"I bet you're real tired of thinkin about it, huh. What'd she need these loans for?"

"To study film," I mumbled.

Doris clapped her hands. "Now that's a genius thing, Kay! You borrowed Grad PLUS Loans to go with her other loans? Now she's some chick with tattoos living in hipster hell and she can't pay you nothing, right? I thought college made you smart."

"You know what, Doris? Some people are creative. They take risks because they have something to say."

"That's not my fault."

I thought about being back in my apartment at 7AM with the phone in my hand, Doris on the other end, barking like a dog. And here she was, standing next to me on the Boardwalk in Atlantic City, where people went every day to lose their money. If coming here to gamble resembled a pilgrimage, what was leaving town with no money called? Is that when you became a *proven loser*? If you include Leenie's PLUS Loans, I'm in that cohort, even if I never put a cent in a slot machine. Doris knows. She's known it for a long time. I looked at her and thought I saw a smirk on her face. I wanted to smack her.

"You aren't mad at me, are you Kay?"

"Ask me later."

"People think you're ripping off the government when you don't pay your student loans. But you're stuck. You can't go bankrupt and write them off like with credit cards. I get that you're over a barrel."

We went by Caesar's casino, which appeared to mimic someone's idea of Roman architecture, followed by another building with a phony Old West look, then a fake 19th Century apartment building with a mansard roof that was quite large. The mimicry wasn't the point. They evoked the past. People that came here probably found the past reassuring. I don't have an opinion.

Doris walked ahead. I was going to remind her that even if I borrowed too much, things were made worse by bad advice I got from people at the call center—who were paid to give good advice, even if they don't benefit beyond the minimum wage they got working at an intolerable job.

I was mad again. How was the loan servicing system put in place? Who was behind this? Could the federal government be making a profit on these loans? Who else profited besides the servicers?

The call center posse might have clues. If they didn't think they were clues, they might not mention them. They might not care, despite anything Doris said. I still didn't know what Doris told the posse about me. She could have said, "I know this reporter chick—she wants to hear stories about the call center." They already seemed to resent Doris because she quit. They could resent me just because I knew her.

I calmed myself. I'd come this far. Settling scores isn't why I came. I had to wait until we could all sit down. If this couldn't happen now, I wanted to make sure it would happen later.

"Shouldn't we get back and find them," I said.

"No, let them gamble. We got time."

"I don't have time, Doris."

"You got all kinds of time."

"I don't have time!"

We walked a little more, then stopped. We saw the lights from another Trump casino, the Trump Taj Mahal, as it appeared in the fog. It was a massive tower but didn't seem real, like it was made out of dingy white Lego bricks, trimmed with red Legos on the side.

The main entrance was on the other side, a block off the Boardwalk, away from the ocean. I wanted to stop in and see who went to this place. The people strolling by looked like tourists, but down at the heels and most likely on their luck. You could walk inside for free, stare at the chandeliers and gaze at the rugs. Wasn't that enough? Apparently not. You had to gamble. You were compelled to gamble. Why walk away with your money when you could leave empty-handed?

There was a wide concrete stairway leading up from the Boardwalk, like a stairway to heaven, to another level of the Taj Mahal, but it was dark at the top. A lower building stood next to the tower that looked like an infidel's vision of a mosque. Red-trimmed minarets covered the building like they'd fallen from the sky. Some were onion shaped, others were conical. They also seemed to mimic a Russian Orthodox church. There were fake balconies about ten feet above the Boardwalk with no entrances. There was a picture of a church in Moscow that I saw recently in a book. I tried to summon it. I couldn't. Maybe that's what this was supposed to suggest.

It looked pagan. It seemed vaguely religious. Either way, this was a place where supplicants came to be received, even if it was by somebody in a rented tuxedo paid by the hour. The minarets were painted red in the shade of a Shriner's fez and I imagined a parade of them tooling by in those little clown cars. Countless people came here who went through life uncounted and unseen. They came with expectations that wouldn't be met. They kept coming back for more.

Doris stopped across from the stairway. She looked up, like she was trying to see into the darkness at the top.

"So what kind of a name is that, Kay. The Taj Mahal? That sounds like a terrorist group, right? Couldn't they pick another name?"

"I don't think the people responsible for this know where the actual Taj Mahal is."

Doris waved her hand. "They're copying Vegas. I'm just glad I don't work at their call center."

"In the hotel?"

"A chick from my high school works here and told me stories about the place. She takes calls when you phone for a reservation and that. When they get a call, they have to say, `Thank you for calling the Trump Taj Mahal, where wonders never cease.' Call after call in the same tone."

"You're not going to visit her?"

"We don't talk about her," Doris clucked. "She's on the outs."

"What happened?"

"I heard she lives in Ducktown, the Italian part. I'm not sayin nothin."

"Didn't this place almost go bankrupt?"

"No, impossible. How could it go bankrupt? Think of all those slots, all those quarters. Let's go find the posse."

"Why's Stella so fixated on Donald Trump?"

Doris shrugged. "Because he makes deals, then borrows money he don't pay back because that's how smart he is. Stella and her whole family are dumb. She thinks she can glom on to what this smart guy does if she hangs around the right places and some of that rubs off on her. Even if you lose the rent money, you still went to this cool casino before you went broke and got to hang out. How come you have to make everything complicated, Kay?"

"Is Stella's mother getting evicted because she blew the rent money at a casino?"

"Don't mention that to Stella. C'mon, I thought you wanted to go."

We turned back. Doris walked ahead. I thought of the rolls of fat around Doris's waist. She was still attractive, fat or no fat. Working out could improve that. It could have no impact at all. There was something crudely—or cruelly—charming about her. There was something madcap about her gait and facial expressions. It didn't seem like an act.

"What Stella said about my father is only the half of it," she said in a half-whisper. "We lived in Allentown where the factory he worked in closed. It's the same factory his father worked in. Everybody knows about Allentown, it was on the news, they wrote a song about it. He bought a truck and got into the moving business, only nobody moves no more. So he just sits in his moving van, I guess. I haven't seen him in a while. The call center hired me and I moved away."

"Did you ever try to talk Stella out of gambling?"

"It's not about gambling, Kay, it's about luck. A lotta times a person's luck is something they're born with and Stella has no luck. If Stella really had luck, we woulda been stuck on the Parkway long enough so we'd say, hey, let's skip the casino and go straight to Stella's mother. Then she'd head back to PA with the money she didn't lose at the slots. She's a proven loser all her life. I've been thinking about ways to change that. My father is different. When he comes here, he wins. That's what he says."

"Why didn't she bring your father along if he's so lucky?"

Doris's voice began to crack. "Cause...my father hit on Stella when she was 13."

"Meaning?"

"Stell came over my house after school a lotta times when I was workin checkout at a supermarket. My father got laid off. He's hangin around the house, she's hangin around." Doris waved her hand. "They got nothin to do. He did more than just hit on her, They went to the bedroom and did certain things. I *know* they did certain things. No matter they did, he got some pussy off her more than once. It was her first time."

"Is there more to this?"

"There's no more to this," she said quickly. "The two families don't know nothing, I'm the only one who knows. I wish I didn't. It made me start to hate my father and I didn't want to. If my sister knew, she'd call the cops cause it's illegal to get sex off somebody 13."

"Older or younger sister? Did she live at home then?"

Doris bit her fingernails. "Stella keeps sayin she gots to get paid. But how? I hate it when she harps on that. My old man was more bad luck for her."

I wanted to pump her, then thought, wait: this is *her father. And* Stella. If she's lying about this, it's bad. If she's telling the truth, it's bad. This was going to have to wait. Stick to the call center.

"Doris—I'm not getting what I came here for."

"You heard Stella's story, right? About Arizona

and that?"

"I wanna hear more from Marge. And Peg and Margot."

"What's wrong with me and Stella? Why do you have to be a freak about it?"

"I want proof that this is happening to other people, not just me. I'd like get a look inside the call center in PA."

"That's over the top. People are gonna get *real* tired of that, Kay. You ask alotta lotta questions with this superior freakin attitude."

"I don't feel superior."

"But you *act* superior and don't play along."

"I came here didn't I? I played along with that."

Doris laughed. "Ok."

"I wish you'd told me about this trip beforehand."

"Ok."

"I would have done that for you."

"K."

"I can prove what took place between us—there's that—but I need a sense of how widespread this is. My resources are limited. But I'd like to see where this all happens—the call center."

"You need Stella for that."

"If I owe her an apology, fine. There's no ill-will."

"What would you do at the call center?"

"I'd like to see a typical day. I'd like to talk to the people who hire and train you."

"You think they're gonna talk to *you*?"

"I have to get their side of the story."

"Remember, I don't work there anymore. Maybe Peg could help."

"I like Peg. When could I talk with her?"

"Maybe later but maybe not. These chicks are livin paycheck to paycheck. They gots to watch their back, too."

"I'd like to talk to your fed-up supervisor."

"I could call him maybe. But I gotta get some, whaddiacall, distance from that place first. I still got issues."

"Like what?"

"A loan."

"Who do you owe money to?"

"That's why I left town and left the state."

"Who do you owe money to?"

"A relative of somebody."

"At the call center?"

"Yeah, them."

"What happened?"

She looked around like we were being followed. "One time I asked HR if they could advance me some pay. The guy there said they don't do advances, but he had a cousin in Delaware that was opening an internet payday loan website. They got rules in Delaware that make it easy. He gives me the web address and says, 'Go online, they'll give you a loan.' So I get on my laptop. They said you get the money in 24 hours."

"I guess there's an unhappy ending?"

Doris's voice dropped to a whisper. "I borrowed $5000—a *lot* for a payday loan. That's more like an installment loan. The money is supposed to be in my bank account next day. I'm gettin antsy cause I don't know how I'm gonna pay it back."

"Why did you borrow so much?"

"What I borrowed was *peanuts* compared to what *you* borrowed, Kay."

I was going to protest. Doris was still whispering. "The next day I had off work. I'm driving along Route 220 in PA in my clunker—which I got rid of—wondering what's up with this loan and stopped at a Wawa store with an ATM near Jersey Shore."

"You came to the Jersey Shore?"

"It's not at the Jersey Shore. This is in Jersey Shore, Pennsylvania. Don't ask me why they named this town *Jersey Shore* when it's in the middle of PA. So I go inside, dip my card and instead of $5000, there's $50,000! They gimme an extra zero! This girly girl gets to *win*!"

"There was a processing glitch?"

Doris draped her arm around me. "Glitch? I'm rich! I'm yelling, I'm screaming! The chick behind the counter goes, 'Darlin, what's wrong, what's wrong!' I'm going, "Everything's *so not wrong!*" I couldn't tell her what happened, though. People get jealous, right? I said, 'Don't worry, this is fate that brang me here. This is now my lucky Wawa. I will send you a card every Christmas. I'll address it to *My Dear Lucky Wawa.*'"

"So somebody wrote some bad computer code and you got an extra $45,000?"

"That's how I financed the move out of PA, darlin. I quit the call center the next day. I shoulda gave them a week's notice but I was afraid that by then the payday lender would find their mistake."

"Are you paying any of it back?"

"Shhh!"

She stopped and looked around again. Her voice returned to a whisper. "I wanted cash. I tried ATMs at Wawa, Kroger's, some banks and that. The max I could get was $350. I did ten $350 withdrawals in an hour before they blocked me from taking more. But I still had $47,000 in the bank. I'd have to make like 170 ATM withdrawals if I wanted all cash. So I went to a teeny tiny bank in PA, wrote a check for the rest, opened an account and boom! It cleared. I'll take that money out and put it in another bank just to be safe."

"I think that's called money laundering, Doris."

Doris was out of breath. "On top of that, I can't believe I got this job typing for lawyers. The computer part is hard but it pays way better than the call center. Queens is expensive, though. I can type 120 words per minute. Everybody knows how to type now, just not that fast. I think it's because of the internet."

She looked over her shoulder again. "What I heard at the call center, Kay, was that a lot of borrowers are scared but a lot say they're *never* gonna pay—they just don't have the money. You're one of the ones who *wanted* to pay. These other people call *me* dirty names, then say they're not payin. I get the reason. The government or a bank loans you a lotta lotta money to go to a crappy school and you don't know how bad it is until it's too late. The school promises you a job but there's no job. It's the schools' fault cause they suck and charge too much. I don't know who's really to blame. Alls I know is I got paid."

"So can I get some phone numbers for Stella and Peg?"

Doris brushed my shoulder, actually gave me a hug. "I'm going to let you in on a little secret, Kay, about why your auto-debit payment didn't work for you."

"You knew something about that? Didn't I ask a million times?"

"When you got bumped from your first servicer to us, the auto-debit deal you did with the first servicer don't go with your loan. That's why your payments didn't go through."

"Why would that happen?"

"No idea. It happens a lotta lotta times."

"Then what?"

"Then your payments don't get made. Then you get calls saying, 'Kay! You're delinquent!'"

"What should I have done?"

"Tell your bank you got a new servicer and set up new auto-debit payments with Fedloan. Now, if we don't tell you about this, you don't know. The fees and interest pile up."

"And that's what happened to me?"

"You're not the only one that lost their auto-debit set up when they got switched to another servicer and their payments didn't post. And got charged fees. Multiply that by a lotta lotta loans and what do you get? Big bucks for somebody. Maybe the servicers, maybe the federal government."

"Don't they train you to prevent this?"

"There's too many calls, we can't keep up."

"Goddam it, people have a right to know these things!"

Doris clucked. "It's the same with applying the payments. If we service more than one loan for you or your daughter, you have to tell us where to put the payments. If you don't, you don't get a say over where the payments go." Doris shrugged. "I have no idea how they decide to apply the payments, but loans get mixed up sometimes. Documents get lost and mistakes get made. Payments get applied in a way that makes the most money for the servicer a lotta times and they do it on purpose."

I heard the ocean. This was starting to sink in. The auto-debit payments weren't made after I got moved from the first servicer to Fedloan. Then when I paid at the website or mailed a check, they posted it to the Stafford Loans, so PLUS wasn't getting paid. Part of me was resisting the idea that this was really happening. Then I was resisting the idea that this was deliberate.

"So you're supposed to tell me all this—and you

didn't?"

Doris put her arm around me. "I swear, Kay, I didn't have a say on nothing at that place. You can fix the auto-debit thing by calling your bank and Fedloan. I forget how you change the payment instructions. It's like Stella said in the car, out of sight, out of mind. Now that I don't work there, I don't think about the call center. There's a lotta stuff about that job I'm forgetting."

I wanted to leave. Find the bus station. Go back and phone the call center, get this loan payment thing fixed. It was Sunday night. Fedloan would be closed until tomorrow.

We kept walking toward Stella's Trump casino. If Stella blew all her money by now, she'd be done with talking. Doris probably did a lousy job of explaining what I wanted. So did I. The heel of my shoe got caught between two planks in the boardwalk. I stopped to pull it out. Doris stopped with me.

"So you wanna get everybody's story, right?"

I was mumbling. "That's where Stella, Peg, Marge and Margot come in."

"How about you?"

"I'll be there to get it all down."

I still wasn't sure Doris knew what this meant. If I told her I wanted to *interview* them, the word *interview* might be the deal breaker. We walked five casinos up the Boardwalk and then went back the other way—from the Trump Taj Mahal to the Sands, the Claridge, Bally's Park Place, Caesar's, then Stella's Trump.

The place was big. The place was dead. There were no clocks. No Stella, Peg, Marge or Margot. The ambient light from the ceiling was dim, made dimmer by the cigarette smoke. Doris showed me Stella's lucky slot machine. The chair in front of it was empty.

We waited. If somebody came and started throwing money in Stella's lucky slot machine and Stella showed, we'd have to pry them apart. Stella wasn't here, though.

"Now what, Doris? We can't do anything until we find them."

"I have this feeling something's up with Stella's mother."

"Is this another omen, Doris?"

"Stella believes in omens, not me. Let's go to the hotel and wait for her there."

"The hotel?"

"We got a hotel. I told you, right?"

"You *told* me, *Doris* that we were going back *tonight!*"

"Hold on, Kay. Stella says what we do. She's drivin."

"You have a rare talent, you know that?"

"A talent for what?"

"Goddam you, Doris!"

"C'mon Kay, you can afford to spend the night here with that money you make writin those genius financial stories. Don't be cheap."

I was silent. I'm just vain enough that I couldn't tell her I make less money than she thinks. I was furious. My default reaction was to get mad.

I started to calm down. If we're all at a hotel, that'll be my chance to talk with them. Stella's car wasn't a good place.

Doris nudged me. "Let's go to the hotel and see if Stella left a message."

"Why didn't you tell me about her mother?"

"Her mother was far away when we left. Now she's not."

I was going to ask why she didn't tell me before

about her father and Stella. Something told me *don't*.

We left the Boardwalk at Bellevue Avenue, a street that began with a ramp beside the Tropicana. Fifty feet later it became a street that could be in Appalachia. Nothing moved. All the houses looked empty and dark. The casinos on the Boardwalk seemed far away. Even though it was the fall it was a warm and muggy night.

The hotel was on Atlantic Avenue among a row of pawn shops and empty store fronts. The elevator didn't work. The room had the rancid odor of a thousand dirty socks, a sign that there was mold or mildew in the air-conditioner, the rugs or mattresses. I had to pee and take off my heels, at least for a few minutes. From the bathroom I could hear Doris checking for messages on the room phone. I pushed the door open a crack.

"That was Stella from a phone booth," she said as I came out. "She's just down the block with the car."

"How much money did she lose?"

"We didn't talk slots. She said for me to come and we'll drive to her mother's."

"How far is it?"

"Depends on how she drives."

I looked at the clock on the night table. "It's late."

"Stella and them might warm up to you more if you went. You could win them over. Why stop now?"

"I have to work tomorrow."

"Call in sick."

There was a cot and two queen beds. I sat on one and put my shoes back on. Peg would get the cot. I wondered where I would sleep if I stayed here. What happened with Stella's mother could go on and on.

"Doris, I don't have a job I can blow off and they'll say, 'Because it's Kay, it's cool.' Because it's me, it won't be cool at all."

"I think hanging out here is your best chance at hearing her story."

We looked at each other and at the paintings in plastic frames on the walls. They reminded me of Margaret Keane's sad-eyed waifs with big eyes and angels with squishy wings. Somebody said her work was naive art. That's not the same as folk art. Were these Keane knock-offs lining the walls of every low-rent hotel in America? There could be thousands of them in warehouses, waiting for more hotels to be built. I couldn't remember where Keane's work first surfaced. It could have been an art gallery. A hotel chain. The ladies' room at a casino. Or on the street.

I didn't know what to do with Doris's father. I wanted to hang that on the wall and come back to it.

"So where's the chicks, Doris."

"There's something about Stella that I forgot."

"What?"

"That I wasn't supposed to tell anyone about my father and her."

"And?"

"I forgot and told you anyways."

"Let's forget about it."

"It's not that simple. I broke a promise. And she's not just my friend, she's my cousin."

I had an inkling Doris was going to reveal something and hold back, reveal and hold back all night. I looked at my watch. It wasn't there.

"If there's something you want to get off your chest, Doris, do it."

"I got it off my chest and I shouldn't have. I shouldn't have told you all that about Stella and my father. That was wrong because she doesn't want anyone to know. Him getting sex off Stella when she was a kid was wrong. I acted like it wasn't."

Doris's father was becoming like Leenie. I wanted to leave him out. I couldn't if he influenced the call center behavior of Doris and Stella. They were like the paintings in the hotel room. I could stare at them all night and they'd have nothing to say.

"Tell me what happened with your father, Doris. Let's get it out."

"I was there a lot of the times when they did it there."

"There?"

"At our house. With me standing outside the door while they were having sex."

"What were you doing?"

"Listening."

"Why?"

"I couldn't believe he was doing this and didn't know what to do. Then I stopped listening. After I stopped listening, I should of stopped this from happening. I should of broke down the door and said Dad! Stop! I just went away instead."

"Then what?"

"I talked to her after. We hugged. A lot."

"Then what?"

"There's a word for what my father didn't get when he was with Stella."

"A word?

"Begins with a C."

"Consent?"

"Yeah, that one."

"But she was underage."

"I thought that when it finally stopped..."

"Did it stop?"

"When she moved away I thought it would stop but it didn't really because he hunted her down. I should of done something but he's really a big huge guy. I regret all that, everything that happened."

Doris was choking on her words. She seemed like Stella coming out of the parking garage. "That's why I called you, Kay. I was looking for someone to talk to about this. I picked you because I liked your picture in that newspaper and I wanted to see what you were like in person. You looked like somebody honest who'd listen. Now that you listened, I wish I hadn't told because now I have to tell Stella that I told you. We made a promise and I broke it. I shouldn't have told."

Doris's father, not student loans, was why I was here. I couldn't turn that off like I couldn't turn the air-conditioner on and it made its own noise. The sympathy I had for Stella was competing with how pissed off I was about being here. Had I seen this movie before? I must have. Why couldn't I remember the ending?

"I need a plan to meet up with the call center people, Doris.

"Come with me to Stella's mother."

"*Doris*...I gotta work tomorrow."

"If you came now, you could hear more from them. That's better than doing it later and you might not get another chance. But Stella gets the say and I gotta run this by her first—that I told you about my father and that."

"How long is that gonna take? Where is she?"

"She's gonna call. Soon."

I punched the air-conditioner button and the motor started. It sounded like a garbage disposal unit. It sputtered and coughed. The phone rang.

"You gonna answer that, Doris?"

Doris picked up the phone. I didn't listen. I wondered where I'd be if I'd gone home after working on a Saturday night. Probably on my laptop, staring at a pixel-packed void.

I thought about old friends, the mothers of my kids' playmates that I'd never see again, especially the ones from when Rod was a child. I thought of swings in a park and pushing Rod on a swing, talking to the parent next to me. I wished I could scare up money for a trip to Denver but they'd all be gone. Hanging with those parents was the high point of my week. But the kids got older and we grew apart. I missed those people and that time and place like I missed Rod the child. Rod the adult I'd have to think about.

If I could get Margot, Peg and Marge into the story, maybe I could skip Stella and Doris—and her father. How bad would it be if I called in sick tomorrow?

Doris hung up. "Stella wants me to meet her."

"Where."

"In the car."

"Let's go."

"No, you wait here."

"No, I'll go."

"You can't go, Kay. Just this once you can't. I gotta clear up what's between her and me. I have to explain what I told you and make her see that it's not so bad—then we're back and you can chat us up all night."

She left. I was alone in the room.

I tried to listen to the phone messages but couldn't. I called the front desk. The desk clerk couldn't help me.

I gave Doris ten minutes. I went down the stairs. I looked up and down the street. No Doris. No Stella. No Crown Vic.

I tried to get back in their room, thinking there'd be phone messages that would tell me something but I couldn't get inside. I thought I convinced the desk clerk to let me in, I almost had him, but he changed his mind. Then he dug in his heels. I left.

I was on a street near the end of the Atlantic City Expressway. It was dark. The street lights were dim and far apart. Where were all the high-rolling gamblers? Why weren't they spilling off the Boardwalk in linen suits and on to the Monopoly board of side streets, looking for their Lincolns and Lexuses? There was almost no one but me.

Things I didn't know before became clearer. Doris explained why the auto-debit payments weren't being made and why the payments weren't going to the PLUS Loans. That was a revelation. That made me furious. Unless it wasn't true or just partly true. It *was* hard to believe. Doris said the posse wanted to talk about the call center. I was lucky they said anything. They said a lot but I didn't know what they were leaving out.

I was starting over, even if I wasn't starting from scratch. I didn't get the name of the law firm where Doris worked or her address, a dumb mistake. The gym was the only place I could find her.

I went back to the hotel, where the desk clerk let me look in some phone books. There was no one listed named Recker. Or Morris.

Doris and Stella were becoming the same person. Doris said they were cousins. Are they lovers? I had to separate them, talk to them alone. Neither of them were here. I thought about what they said in the car after I nodded out. The hum of the road put me to sleep. Once a week I nod out at my desk.

Someone tapped me on the shoulder. It was the desk clerk. He wanted his phone books. Then he said don't come back.

Street signs pointed the way to the bus station. I followed them. For all the lights that turned the sky gauzy, the streets of Atlantic City were bleak at night. I didn't see anyone who looked like they came for sun and fun. People looked hostile. On one block I walked through the middle of a drug deal.

I thought about going back to the hotel. I could look for a bar and hang out until I saw them, even if I was up half the night. There was no bar. Instead I found a casino excursion bus going straight to the George Washington Bridge. That settled it.

I got a window seat about 20 rows from the front next to someone whose face I couldn't see. The bus was on the outskirts of town going north. Everyone sat up wide-eyed as though they were counting the money they no longer had.

After the bus turned north on to the Parkway I smelled dope coming from the back, too far for the driver to notice but close enough for me to get high. It wouldn't do to make a scene. Then what? The driver pulls over, he calls the state troopers and we're sitting there until the small hours of the morning. Instead I sat there inhaling all this smoke. If second-hand tobacco smoke is harmful, it must be the same with dope. It drifted over my seat like a cloud. Soon I'd be buzzed.

That brought me to an uncomfortable place for most of the ride. I should have stayed in Atlantic City, even for one night. I should have gone with Doris to see Stella's mother. I could play it by ear with Stella. I could play it by ear with Doris. If the tourist season was over, I could have gotten a room and made an excuse at work. It was too late to fret about being part of the story. I'd already crossed that fake Rubicon. I thought about what I had.

First there were the student loans. They were driving people to ruin and the servicers were making things worse while they made money off this. There were the PLUS Loans for my daughter that let you borrow more than you could repay. And there's me, the co-signer, and the federal government, the lender. Only the payments weren't being made when I sent the servicer money.

That led to Doris who told me what I should have already known—that student loan servicing was a con job. There was Doris at the gym. How did we end up in the same gym? Stella would say "That's an omen!"

Next came the call center posse. These same people drove to Atlantic City to gamble and went to this town where Stella's mother was getting evicted. Tomorrow they could be standing on a street with no sidewalk as Stella loaded her mother into the Crown Vic and the outraged posse went home on a bus. The call center chicks, who hounded borrowers, were broke themselves. Except for Doris. The editor of that new news website might lose interest once she saw what I had. I might have to get real creative to make this work. The story about Doris's father would follow me home.

The posse could be gone in a month. Doris left, the others could scatter like the people they were trying to collect from. What about Doris's $50,000 payday loan she got by accident? Do I believe that? It was part of the story whether she was lying about it or telling the truth.

Borrowing and gambling didn't seem so far apart. Both were trafficking in the hope that things will get better. Life was good, or bearable, until the payments came due. Then let's say you go to a casino believing that if you scored at the slots you'd repay the loan faster. If you put a coin in a slot machine and got nothing, you could trick yourself into thinking that you got closer to pay dirt with each coin, even if you were really getting further away. You put in another. Then another.

I wanted somebody else's point of view. I could ask Lenny, my editor at *SIN* but this wasn't a *SIN* story. There was the editor of the new news website, but that might be a touch awkward since I wasn't sure what I had. I was reluctant to call my son. Calling Leenie was out. I wanted to ask Geoff what he thought but he was gone.

I thought of what he left behind. A pair of gray Tommy Hilfiger boxer shorts appeared in my chest of drawers. An unused condom, still in its wrapper. I found an argyle sock under the bed and one paperback book, *A Room of One's Own* by Virginia Woolf. Was it Woolf or D.H. Lawrence? I read it in college. I don't know what people think of it now and I can't remember much about it. I didn't think of it as a conversation-starter. He did.

One night we were in bed. I'm on my laptop when that book appeared from under the covers like his cock when it got hard. I was determined to work that night but he opened this book. Finally I said "So why are you reading that? He gave me a Cheshire cat smile and replied, "I wanted to impress you." I was going to ask him what kind of impression he thought he'd make. I never asked. It's too late now. I have a room of my own again. Funny, I never thought of it as Geoff's room. But when he was there it wasn't completely mine.

I wondered if I wasn't doing a variation on the room-of-one's-own concept. Or doing something other people already tried. Instead of a room of one's own, how about a bed of one's own?

You mean a bed of one's own?

Yes, a bed. You could still have sex. It can be a single or a king, but nobody sleeps there but you. A room of one's own doesn't go far enough.

That's not for everyone and it isn't anything I'm wedded to. Sometimes I'm bitter. Sometimes I can't get off on sex that much anymore. At first I thought I'm too much of a physical specimen for this to be physical. That could be wrong.

But there's nothing wrong with my health and I'm not on performance enhancing drugs or any meds. So why does my sex drive sometimes leave me? It would be there at the start, then peter out. I decided that pushing myself at the gym was part of it. But if it wasn't, how would I know? If it was my own quirky physiology I wouldn't know that either. I'm not ready to say that it's my age. There were glitches in that other sex organ, my head, although I can be so horny at times. It's what people say when we're having sex that can ruin it for me. It's hard not to listen. Your ear can be right next to their mouth. Why am I thinking about this and not Stella?

There was a time I was doing it with Geoff, not long before he left. He was really getting into it. I was thinking of all the pushups I can do, but I couldn't really get wet. There was a tube of KY on the night table. It stayed there. I tried to fit my finger into a place between me and where his cock was going in to help this along.

It didn't work. It wasn't uncomfortable, it was kind of blah. I stared at the ceiling in the way that millions of women stare at the ceiling. Then I said, "I'm not gonna cum. Can you finish?"

This wasn't really about him and it wasn't anything new. Something similar is probably said every day, every night of the week, across borders, languages, cultures and income brackets. Or it's in the minds of millions of women who'd had their genitals cut as girls and wouldn't dare say anything out loud, who'd risk life and limb if they complained. In some places it's probably never even discussed because you can't. With me, it's rarely said because I don't want to hurt anyone's feelings. Just don't try to force me to do something I don't want to because I'll smack you one.

With Geoff, I made it clear, in so many words, gestures, tones of voice, that this wasn't his fault. But when we were doing it he kept saying: oh, god. That's all he could say, oh god, over and over. He didn't always say it but when he did it was such a turn off. Or oh...*God*. Or *Oh Gawd* because of that accent of his. Or Oh GAWD! Oh GAWWWWWD! Oh GAWWWWD! Oh GAWWWWWWD!

Geoff was very spirited which was fun. But I kept muttering over and over *I'm not god, I'm Kay.* That left me lying there, trying to remember the people who went oh, god, oh, god, oh, god, oh, god—and this is like 30 years' worth of people. Who was this god? Was it a universal god? Their own private god? The god of their gonads? A god from hell? An undiscovered god who was just around the corner, a god-in-waiting? If he would just stop saying *oh, god* I'd be fine. Or better.

Once when he was on an Oh Gawd tear I said, "What's my name?" He was on the verge of getting his rocks off and I guess he couldn't force those words out. I tried again before I said, "If you're going to say how grateful you are, could you try addressing *me*, since without *me* you wouldn't be here? Do you think that you could, just once, say: Oh, Kay? God didn't bring you here. *I* did." I can't remember what he said.

If you stop and listen, if you put your ear to the ground or the floor of this casino bus, you can almost hear it, going out to the ends of the earth, like a voice echoing from a mountain top. *Oh, god.* At times, when I'm on my back, staring at the ceiling, a guy on top of me, all this can feel profound. Later, when I'm standing on the A train holding on to a pole, avoiding the eyes of a stranger, it seems so banal. Why is that?

These thoughts came hurtling at me like traffic on the southbound lanes of the Garden State Parkway. Headlights bobbed in the dark, then flew behind me. I was definitely stoned. I thought of my son Rod's father and Leenie's father, like they were two distant vehicles fleeing the scene of an accident. The headlights made me think of the student loan experts I hadn't met yet who could help me get this story right. There was a lot I had to learn that would take time I didn't have. But if there was something to be written about this that could help shed light on dark places—how could I just give up?

The bus got to New York sooner than I expected. It went passed the bus station beneath the GW Bridge and parked on Ft. Washington Avenue. I saw some of my dispirited fellow travelers for the first time as they stumbled onto the sidewalk and looked, as Stella would say, like proven losers. The streets of Washington Heights were not as dark as Atlantic City, but they were dark. The walk to my building seemed longer. I blamed it on these stupid shoes. The elevator seemed more cramped. My apartment looked smaller.

There were no phone messages, which made me feel lonely. That meant no messages from Fedloan, either. Or Leenie. It was past dinner time in LA. She'd have eaten dinner at a strange dinner table, one I wouldn't recognize. When I went into the bathroom, Geoff's toothbrush was still there.

I walked into her room and sat down on the bed. My son Rod didn't leave much behind when he moved out. Most of what was still there was Leenie's. The work bench where she refurbished shoes was really an old table with a vise and some tools. It looked the way it did when she left. I picked up an unfinished shoe she was working on. The instep side was untouched, but the other side was filled with an elaborate cartoon that was like a tattoo. It was unlike her to leave something unfinished. I tried to remember her state of mind when she left for California. Was she hopeful? Anxious? This unfinished shoe wasn't helping me remember.

Leenie and Rod slept in bunk beds. They liked each other as kids, even if they drifted apart. He usually took the bottom, but sometimes they'd switch and not tell me. I sat down and worried that she wouldn't know a lost cause when she saw one. I worried again that she should be designing shoes instead of trying to get a job in film and that she should be anywhere but in film.

When my daughter was in middle school I told her to follow her dreams. That was a long time ago. I can't remember what her dreams were then. They must have been the dreams of a child.

Chapter Five

By the time I fell asleep it was Monday. When I sleep, it's a numb, deep sleep. When I woke up and looked at the ceiling I saw an eviction notice taped to the door where Stella's mother lived. I looked at my arm. Stella's license plate number was there but some of the numbers had rubbed off. I couldn't read it. I wondered where Doris's father was.

I thought of calls I had to make because of yesterday. It was 5 AM. I e-mailed Fedloan about the auto-debit payment. I still had to phone my bank.

I left before the phone could ring. When *SIN* hired me I dressed up—stockings and a tailored skirt. Gradually I skipped the stockings, lost the skirts. There was never an announcement, but everyone eventually went casual. The only thing left from before was some lip gloss and a touch of eye makeup. I have some blemishes. They're manageable. A sign on the back of my apartment door says *Don't forget your keys.*

Grace Fong, who lived across the hall with Wensi Fong, was standing in her doorway.

"Hello, Grace."

"Kay—don't go away."

She ducked inside. I could hear Wensi's voice. I was still stoned from last night's bus ride. Being stoned kept me from feeling tired.

I hadn't seen Grace in weeks. The door opened and a guy carrying a raincoat walked out. She followed him.

"Kay, this is my *friend*, Glen. Want to walk to the

train with us?"

I fumbled with my keys while they headed to the elevator. They waited. She held the door and we got in.

"Have a late night out, Kay?"

"Why do you ask?"

"I heard you when you came in."

"Did I make that much noise?"

Grace cleared her throat. "No. We were still up."

Grace wouldn't look at me, not unlike the way Wensi wouldn't look at me that last time I saw her, also in this elevator. "I'm Kay," I said to the guy. "Come here much?"

"Yep. I mean nope."

They both stared straight ahead. At the lobby Grace ran off the elevator like somebody was chasing her. The guy, Glen, followed her. I followed Glen.

The crowd in the station grew. After I got on the A train there was Grace near the middle of the car. She was alone, leaning against a door. A stop later I noticed Glen standing by himself at the other end. They seemed to become strangers when they might know each other well after a certain fashion.

I met Grace first, Wensi later. I met their other roommate, Tia, exactly once. I thought of Grace's remark about having a late night out. Not long after they moved in Grace started having late nights out, then Wensi. They began doing it at home. Men would come late at night and an hour later I'd hear them in the hallway.

Looking at Grace and Glen I was seized by the urge to meddle. I didn't want to be a stranger on the A train when we were neighbors. There was a touch of awkwardness. That wouldn't change this morning. At 145th Street I got a seat. I was pivoting toward work.

But I forgot to bring anything to read again. All I

had was Grace and Glen to distract me. They were still on my mind after they disappeared in the crowded subway car.

There were five apartments on my floor. When I moved in with Leenie and Rod, the Klugers, Esther and Art, lived in the one across from us. They rarely left. Both used a walker. A neighbor said they were married. Somebody else said that they were siblings. I could count on both hands the number of times I saw them. They were in their 90s and after 60 years on Ft. Washington Avenue, they died during the same week.

Their deaths became an event. The cops, the fire department, people from a synagogue and a local politician came. A reporter from the *New York Post* showed up and didn't like the quote I gave him. He wouldn't take "I didn't know these people very well" for an honest answer. I said, "Make up your own quote if you don't like it." The Klugers' relatives arrived with armloads of food and there was a religious observance. It was fraught. I didn't want to interfere.

After the apartment was empty, Grace and Wensi appeared in the hallway carrying boxes. I said hello and figured I wouldn't get to know them either and probably wouldn't have were it not for their cat. The door to their apartment would drift open unless you slammed it. Mine was the same. We'd all forget and their cat kept getting out and sneaking into my place. I'd find it, knock on their door and hand it back to them.

One night I found the cat in the hallway and followed it inside their place. The floor was parquet wood, like mine. The molding along the ceiling was the same kind I had. Grace Fong was sitting alone at the dining room table with a pile of student loan documents and a calculator. My eye went to her calculator. It was just like mine.

Grace was the taller one. Her black hair was twisted into a pony tail. I sat with her while she did the math on her student loans and she was teary-eyed. It was like crunching Leenie's numbers. $140,000 in loans divided by a four-year NYU fine arts degree won't go, she said. It won't go anywhere. It goes down a black hole and takes you with it. She talked about being trapped by these loans forever, at least during her peak earning years, assuming she had them. Before I left I said, "Cheer up, maybe it's not that bad."

I was reluctant to tell them about Leenie's loans. They didn't become less friendly after I did, but from then on they looked at me differently. It was like they thought *oh, so she's like us.* After a while, misery doesn't love company. It wants to be left alone. I know what Manny the super would do if they got a fourth roommate to help with the rent. He'd look the other way like he wouldn't with Geoff. Manny seemed to have a lot of influence over who moved in. He wasn't the super when I came here. I don't know who owned the building.

Later, I was visiting Grace after their cat turned up in my bathtub. I was leaving when she said, "Did you ever think about quitting your job for something that was like, alternative? An alternative kind of job?"

"What do you mean?" I said.

"I say I'm in the art world since I work in a gallery. You could also say I'm a carpenter because a thing I do is make wooden frames for paintings and help a FedEx guy load them on a truck. So if I went into a line of work that most people *wouldn't* call art, but *I* decided that it's art, I'm like an alternative artist then, right? I'd be making a lot more money, too."

"What kind of job is it?"

"A job I'm going to call art. A lot of people would say it's not artistic at all."

"What's the job?"

"A non-art job. But I'm going to say it's art."

"You lost me, Grace."

"I've never done this before. I don't know how to explain it."

I was feeling tired. "If you'd like to save this for later, Grace, it's fine."

Wensi came in with laundry and dropped it on the floor. She peered at Grace. "Have you been telling Kay about the art job?"

"No."

"I wish you wouldn't."

"She didn't tell me, Wensi. And I gotta go."

"Thanks," she said. "I'm expecting a call from my mother, where I'll dodge all the questions that you'd ask me about the art job."

I left. I remembered that they were both from Monterey Park, California, a suburb of LA and that they went to the same high school. I thought of the phone calls with Leenie, where the day had to be rearranged because we're bi-coastal. The cat got out. It spent the night at my place.

The next morning there was a knock on my door. I picked up the cat and was ready to hand it over to Grace or Wensi. There was no one there. I peeked into the hallway. A pale-faced man in a blue leisure suit was standing off to the left. He looked at me and looked at his phone.

"You don't look anything like the photo on the website," he said.

"Pardon me?"

"I'm looking for Grace. Are you Grace?"

"No."

"Then who are you? Another fake provider from a fake website?"

"What?"

He held up his phone. "Where's Grace?"

Doris startled me.

I didn't slam the door in his face. Instead, I pointed to her door across the hallway. After he went inside, I had second thoughts running all over the hallway. I should have asked how he got into the building. I should have told him to fuck off. Grace probably buzzed him in and he went to the wrong door. Our doors were identical and had no apartment numbers. I kept the cat for another hour. Grace came and snatched it out of my hands.

The sex industry had come to my building. I'd had an inkling before. I didn't know if all three of them were doing this or just Grace and Wensi. I resisted the idea, even after the signs were there, because they didn't say anything to me—but why would they? Then Grace told me about her art job.

It seemed a little early for them to be in trouble with their loans, but they were both already in repayment. I fretted about this when I saw them. I fretted about it when someone rang the buzzer to my apartment, thinking it was one of their johns, clients, hobbyists, whatever they're called now. I wanted to chat with them about this. The idea that my advice wouldn't change anything stopped me. They were discrete. They were furtive. It was out in the open, too.

I got off at Fulton Street in Lower Manhattan. The office was another 15 blocks downtown, where Broadway comes to an end across from the Staten Island Ferry. One moment I felt anxious, then relieved. My job at this newspaper was still waiting for me for another week. There's a desk with a plastic plaque that has my name on it, a place where I belong. At least a place where a handful of people expect to find me. The idea that I *belong* there doesn't sit right. Sometimes I have to work at being the person who works at this job. Today it was enough that I still had one.

The street was pretty empty. After I went a block down Broadway I saw my boss, Lenny Shrank, editor-in-chief of *SIN*, not far in front of me. Even with his back to me in the dark, I still knew it was him.

Sometimes Lenny looked like Yoda, down to his scaly complexion and reptilian eyes. Sometimes his head was like the hood ornament on a car from the early days of cars. Then he seemed steely, stoic. You often couldn't see it because he wore some kind of hipster fedora, but from before they became cool. The whole hipster look seemed like an imitation of Lenny. It wasn't. He still got there first by a couple of decades.

I was around Lenny more than anyone I knew. When I caught a glimpse of him on Saturday I thought it was better if we *didn't* see each other at work for a change. I wanted to walk the rest of the way alone to clear my head. After I got there I'd wait for him at the security desk. He could sign me in. I forgot my badge.

But what was he doing? He was standing by the curb, bending over a trash can. He had his hands in it, rummaging around. I doubt if he was looking for an ineffable answer to a burning question. Although with Len you never knew.

I stood against a construction hoarding and waited. After he stood up I walked over. When I got close I gasped. His hat and his hair were gone.

"Oh, god, Lenny, you shaved your head!"

He shrugged. "It didn't shave itself."

"And you're wearing earrings? What happened?"

"Nothing yet. Why are you up so early, Kay?"

"I couldn't sleep."

"Ah, sleep. It's like a forbidden elixir, isn't it?"

His coat covered up a paunch which made me think of a medicine ball. I imagined poking it. Would it be hard, like something filled with water, or soft, like a pillow? He was a little over weight, but that seemed separate from his distended belly that bulged like an appendage. If he was sitting behind his computer, it would be hidden under his desk. When he stood up, there it was again.

Lenny was silent. He walked very slowly.

"Why are *you* up so early, Len?"

"What makes you think I'm up?"

He often answered a question with another question when he thought your question wasn't worth answering. Then your question would be left hanging. It was the kind of thing that made me irate coming from anyone else.

We were coming to a clot of people who were milling around and not going anywhere, near the edge of Zuccotti Park on Broadway. It was where the Occupy Wall Street demonstrators put their stakes in the ground, actually two or three blocks from Wall Street, and began their occupation which went beyond this global, insular neighborhood. It seemed to start as a protest against, well, Wall Street, drawing on the 2008 financial crisis among other things. It got bigger. People who joined seemed to come from nowhere. Whenever I walked by it reminded me that things were bad. It also reminded me that they were going to have to fold their tents, probably another sign that things were bad.

We came to the edge of a curb. There was a critical mass of people that changed shape and kept us from moving. The sound rising from the park was hard to describe. It was diffuse but coming from the same place. It was hard to see how far the crowd went and where it petered out.

"Let's cross the street," I said. "Let's check out Occupy Wall Street."

"Too many people," Len said. "I don't think we could go beyond the margins."

"Couldn't we go around to the back?"

I could feel Lenny shake his head. "Don't you have a web story to file about multi-asset class trading that should have gone up last week?"

"I know. I'm so sick of that."

A wedge of people cut in front of us. More were surging on both sides.

"I hate to say this, Kay, but multi-asset class trading will be here a year from now. I don't know about Occupy Wall Street."

"What if they don't go away?"

"That would be an accomplishment. But I'm not sure it's something they can accomplish."

"What if these Occupy people can have some influence later, after it's over?"

"After *what* is over? And what do you mean by later? Suppose your kids are doing this ten years from now? Or if not them, your grandkids? What if Lower Manhattan is under water after the polar ice caps melt and they can't pitch a tent here?"

The milling throng seemed to speed up, like they were moving a little faster inside the park, which was below the sidewalk level of Broadway. A few more steps and we seemed to enter a different country. You could almost look down into it. But it was dark. You couldn't see how far it went.

Most of the tents were orange, bunched together so that you couldn't see the ground which was concrete or something hard. How could you pitch a tent on it?

Had there been a revolution in tent design? People who were respectable, who had jobs they could lose any minute, could walk by, eyeball the crowd and see themselves there.

I nudged Lenny. "Maybe we should go across the street and try to talk to some of the demonstrators."

Lenny was silent. I couldn't see his face.

"Really, Lenny, we should get something in the newspaper about this, even if it's small."

"It doesn't synch with the editorial calendar."

"It synchs with my secret plan to break you out of the rut you're in. Let's go see where they're at."

"I don't have time. And they're mostly kids."

"Come on, Len, youth must be served."

"I don't know what service I could provide. And I don't feel particularly old. At least I didn't use to."

I was distracted as the crowd roared. It was a little like being in a stadium. "You what?"

"Although, if I had my druthers, I'd run a story where we interview somebody from a big broker dealer who maligns *Big Government* and ask what they think about the government's plan buy mortgage-backed securities that have become worthless. How bad does *Big Government* look then?"

"Let's do it."

"I don't have my druthers."

"Sure you do."

"Or, I'd run a statement by somebody from a bank complaining about the corporate tax rate. Next to it I'd put numbers describing that bank's dive into the subprime lending and how tax payers bailed them out."

"I like it."

"I think you better stick to ops and technology, Kay. We're the trade press and live inside our own little bubble."

"What about compliance and regulation? We cover that, too."

"The word from management is to lighten up on regulation and emphasize technology. This isn't my idea. At least you're not saying let's write about the Arab Spring."

I mentioned that last week, so mea culpa. Some people compared Occupy Wall Street to the Arab Spring. That was turning into something that could resemble a nuclear winter. At the same time there were not one but two wars going on. One was supposed to be ending. Both could continue in a different form after they were supposedly over. They could end and begin again. They could be fought almost anywhere by almost anyone. There were people in office buildings not far from here thinking of ways to promote idea that the universe was unfolding as it should because they have products to sell.

I was thinking about my desk on the 22nd floor, where I was afraid I'd start to nod out before noon. Even though I slept, I woke up too early. Then I couldn't stay in bed fighting the pillows, it was like being attacked by marshmallows, poking me here, poking me there. I wanted that hard desk top under my elbows before I could start thinking about the inevitable: multi-asset class trading. I had written over 50 stories about that, many more than anyone needed. I'd finish one, then lose sight of the fundamentals because I was resisting the idea of writing another. When the time came, I'd have to call my sources again and wheedle explanations about things they'd already explained.

More people were clogging the streets around the Occupy site. There was an opening and I nudged Lenny forward. We moved toward a space in the park. Cops in riot gear got there first. One had his plastic face shield in my face.

"You can't go beyond here," he said.

"Why?"

"On account of all these people, keep it movin, you're blockin the flow."

"We want to be in the flow."

"The flow left without you."

"No, it's still here."

"It just left," the cop said. "Look but don't touch."

People pushed us. We're stumbling around in the dark, going the way the cop pointed us, away from Broadway. Somebody shoved me from behind and we were surrounded. A bunch of kids with buzz cuts threw me into Lenny who was giving ground but not fast enough and we were spun into a line of people who fell like bowling pins. I was flat on the sidewalk. My legs got tangled up underneath me. Len helped me to my feet.

We were back on Broadway, heading downtown. Across the street the police occupied the curb lane in front of 120 Broadway which they used as a staging area for traffic stops. Somebody told me they'd been there since 9/11, which was a year or two before I came here. *SIN's* office was near Penn Station then. It was a while before I actually set foot on Wall Street.

A crush of people appeared. Lenny wasn't going so slowly this time. He lowered his shoulder and moved through the crowd. We left the block the park was on and got to a clearing by the curb. We stopped and looked back.

"So why don't we occupy Wall Street, Len? Just for a while."

"I'm too late for that party." A roar rose from the crowd that almost drowned out his voice.

"How do you mean?"

"Haven't we been through this before, Kay?"

I paused for a moment. "You're right—we have. It's not a party, though."

"I've been here for going on 30 years," he said. "Wall Street occupies me, I can't occupy them. They've owned my life, even if that didn't happen right away. I've been devoted to a lot of worthless crap, as you know. Think of Y2K."

"I never think of Y2K."

"Right, you were in Round Rock, Texas then."

"I was never in Round Rock, Texas."

"Wherever you were, you weren't around when those digits turned from 2000 to 1999. Crazed COBOL programmers thought the earth would spin off its axis."

"It worked out eventually, right?"

"Before it did, the banks had to justify the Y2K spend by hyping this into a crisis. They needed the media and I took the bait. Then at midnight those two digits flipped over in every time zone. 2000 became 1999 like it was the most ordinary thing in the world. Instead of working on weekends, I could have stayed home eating chocolate bon bons."

There was something that was *off* here. "Wait, Lenny. I think those digits went from 1999 to 2000, not 2000 to 1999."

"No, it was 00 to 99. Trust me, I was there with crazed code monkeys."

I did trust Lenny. He was practically a Y2K authority even though there was practically no story in the end. So how could he confuse 1999 with 2000? It was too early. He needed some bon bons.

"Yeah, well, Wall Street occupies me, too, if you put it that way," I said. I didn't want to put it that way. I hated being occupied by Wall Street.

Lenny's glasses slid to the end of his nose. "This Occupy thing has to monetize itself if it wants to keep going. That's the way this country works for better or worse. They need a thing, a commodity."

"Maybe somebody's working on it."

"How about Occupy Wall Street Food Co-ops. Or OWS Pre-Schools. What about an Occupy Wall Street debit card with cash back rewards?"

"Who would underwrite it?"

"No one. And this whole thing could have been avoided. No one knew that the Bear Stearns failure was the beginning of a global crisis, not the end of one investment bank. Bear blew up in March, Lehman didn't fail until September while the short sellers had their knives out all summer. Wall Street and the government had seven months to get this right."

We still re-hashed the financial crisis mainly because it will never end for many people. Lenny said it was avoidable, I said it wasn't. It reminded me that we were as close to anyone who made decisions about this as cornstalks on a field in Kansas. If we seemed to be grasping at straws, so did the government officials who bristled at the idea that they did anything wrong.

Bear Stearns was one of Len's obsessions. Bear survived the 1929 stock market crash and the Great Depression but not 2008. And lest we forget, many of the seeds were sown over a decade before when Brooksley Born, Bill Clinton's futures regulator, got bitch slapped by her male colleagues for suggesting that the derivatives market should be better regulated.

Supposedly Clinton wanted her back for his second term but she left. I couldn't dig into anything like that. We've been writing more about what code developers do than regulators. Trade data got priority.

I came to appreciate Len's Bear Stearns fixation. The Securities and Exchange Commission formed something called the Consolidated Supervised Entities

Program. The big investment banks—Bear Stearns, Goldman Sachs, Lehman Brothers, Merrill Lynch and Morgan Stanley—all joined. It was a sleight of hand that let them to do business in the European Union but also allowed them to regulate themselves. They borrowed huge sums to invest in asset-backed and mortgage-backed securities that became nearly worthless and crashed the market. That's part of what this road to hell was paved with.

The banks were no different, Len said, from somebody who borrowed too much against the equity in their house before property values crashed. I said the banks were much worse. They pushed people into loans they didn't understand and couldn't repay, then demanded bailouts from the government when the borrowers defaulted. The banks got paid, the borrowers got played. Countless people lost everything. Somebody somewhere must know how much.

Len thought Bear Stearns was the smoke that led to the fire. He hated it if you weren't overcome by the same smoke.

"Bear's prime brokerage and clearing business should have been worth *something*, Len. Didn't they own a lot of real estate?"

"It couldn't help them. This was like a bank run, a panic. Bear was insolvent. When it was over, the word on The Street was that the government would support the banks' balance sheets from then on. But they let Lehman fail. Another 500 banks failed. If they'd been smarter, none of these demonstrators would be here. All those people wouldn't have been thrown out of their houses. There'd be no debt crisis. We wouldn't be worried about our jobs."

"Who in journalism wasn't already worried?"

Len didn't reply. I thought back to when I was

Wonder Woman with no debt. That's over. I not only borrowed thousands of dollars in student loans, I borrowed $20 from Grace Fong.

Last summer I was in the subway and forgot my wallet. Grace walked by. I said, "Hey Grace, can you lend me a swipe from your MetroCard?"

She had one left. Even if she swiped me in, I'd still need a MetroCard to get home. We emptied our handbags. Grace turned up a $20 bill. I said I'd pay her back that night.

But when I got home, I only had $25 on me. I couldn't bear to give up everything but those last five bucks. Instead of knocking on their door I looked to see if there was some money stashed somewhere in my apartment. The phone rang. I was distracted.

This went on for weeks. Every time I stopped to get money for her, I had almost nothing in the bank. Once I had thousands of dollars in my savings account. Whenever I went to withdraw 20 bucks for Grace, I found that the well had almost run dry.

I thought there must be some sofa cushions or a cookie jar where I stashed some cash. There wasn't. By then Geoff was around. I could have asked him and didn't. To my shock, I couldn't cough up a lousy $20. Leenie had a money crisis, now I had one, too. I didn't realize this was happening. Once I did, I couldn't stop it.

There was something else I keep forgetting. Last winter I had a sebaceous cyst removed from my neck. They're benign and non-cancerous—something for people on the A train to stare it. At the hospital they advised me to stay overnight. I took their advice. When it was over, I got a bill for $3400. My health insurance plan has a $3500 deductible. Pretty soon I was getting a new hit to my bank account every month. That was helping the student loan push me toward the edge.

One morning I saw Grace in the hallway. By then the gentlemen callers were turning up. I went back inside, grabbed $10 out of Geoff's wallet and caught up to her at the elevator. When we got on I handed her the money. "I'll give you the rest later," I said. Grace was silent.

I apologized. I walked with her to the train. She was still silent. Something was off, so I threw in some advice. "Look," I said, "I've seen the men going in and out of your apartment. I know you've got loans and the job market sucks, but is this really a great idea? Maybe you shouldn't put yourself in such a compromising position."

Grace was circumspect but very cordial from the first time we met. In less than a block she went from reserved to really mad. "Did you say that I shouldn't *put myself* in this position? Please, I didn't get here alone. I had plenty of help from higher ed administrators who were so engaged, so *concerned* about my education when I came here. But they've moved on. Now Sallie Mae is the john. NYU is my pimp. I'm their bitch. I've come this far, what if having a covered cock in your mouth isn't much different from having a rubber dildo or somebody's big toe? That's how I rationalize this. I'm doing this even if I can't rationalize it. This doesn't define me. When it's time to end it, it'll end. And if you look, there's a market for Asian chicks."

"Grace..."

"And by the way, it took a *month* for you to pay me back—and you still owe me $10. What's *your* problem?"

She got on the train and went to the other end of the car, not unlike this morning. She didn't mention an art job. Or the art of being a provider.

The guy I saw Grace with this morning was about her age. That made me think that he wasn't a john or a hobbyist, that he was a boyfriend. But he probably wasn't. He was her user, she was his provider. If she was afraid that he was going to give her a hard time, she wanted a witness, somebody she knew, in case something happened. That's why she held the elevator for me this morning. Or not.

When will these gentlemen callers go from their side hustle to a full-time job to a criminal enterprise that made them the victims of human trafficking? Grace insisted she was doing this of her own free will but I'm on the lookout for pimps. I might not recognize them. I didn't know how much closer this was coming to the day when I could walk into the hallway and find something I couldn't just walk away from coming out of their apartment. It wouldn't be the cat.

I thought about how Grace and Wensi ended up moving next to me. It was a coincidence. But debt sometimes seemed like a virus. If you know someone with it, could you get it, too? Leenie got one loan, then I got another kind of student loan for her that I co-signed. I think Grace said she was current on her loan when she came to my building. After she moved in, she wasn't current anymore. But it's a coincidence. Debt couldn't be contagious. It was a silly idea, seriously.

Lenny was talking, thinking that I was listening while I was 200 blocks uptown, waiting for the elevator with Grace.

"I'm sorry, Len—what were you saying?"

He looked at me, then waved his hand. "Skip it."

"I got distracted. So what happens to all those bad mortgages? Will banks have to bite the bullet?"

"It'll be more like biting a Hostess Twinkie.

Somebody will pick up a lot of those houses for a song and flip them when the market heats up. This won't end until the private sector starts lending again. The thing that caused the crisis will be the thing that ends it. In the end, it'll be an opportunity for the super-rich to become even richer."

Len pushed his glasses off the end of his nose again. "If people could just stay in their homes, isn't that the best solution? Seriously, go occupy some foreclosed houses. There couldn't be more than 100,000 people in Occupy Wall Street and there are millions of houses that are vacant. Where'd all those people go? On whose couch are they sleeping?"

"Yeah, but how would you get the utilities turned on? Who pays the taxes? Suppose drug dealers squat next door instead of cool political activists?"

"Do you get to choose who your neighbors are, Kay?"

"I've thought enough about my neighbors for one morning. Let's stop for tea."

"I don't drink tea anymore."

"Since when?"

He didn't answer. There was something *off* about Lenny today. It wasn't just earrings and no hair, which he was already losing. He wouldn't look at me. I was interrupting something when we met, although I can't imagine what. He seemed withdrawn on one hand, agitated on the other.

"Hey, Lenny, let's come back here after work and join the Occupy Wall Street clean-up crew?"

"And clean up what?"

"I read that the city thinks Zuccotti Square has become a health hazard. If it's cleaned up maybe they can stay."

"I didn't hear that."

"I could clean up Zuccotti Square instead of my apartment."

Lenny was silent. I nudged him. "Bloomberg, our billionaire mayor, is suddenly concerned about the dirt from Occupy Wall Street. Too funny, right?"

Len didn't reply.

"My subway station in Washington Heights has rats and dirt from the first LaGuardia Administration. Now they're worried about dirt?"

I thought I heard Lenny sigh. It could have been ambient noise from the street. For a moment it didn't seem like we were going to work.

Lenny plunged his hands into his pockets. I was suddenly fixated on cleaning up Zuccotti Park and bringing him with me. I was giddy from no sleep.

"Let's come back and check it out. Are you doing anything later?"

"Actually, I am."

"I'll bet our readers—"

"You *can't* write about Occupy Wall Street, Kay! It's not what we do!"

Lenny slowed down.

"Ok, Len. Suppose you had a wish list of anything you could cover. What would be on it?"

"I can't cover anything anymore."

"What do you mean?"

"I'm leaving town."

"What for?"

"For good."

"What? Why?"

"I have early onset Alzheimer's disease."

"Who does?"

Len's face was partly in shadow, but I could see it go slack. "It's just you and me here, Kay, and if it's not you, who's left?"

My feet were feeling around for the sidewalk. "You have that? Since when?"

He didn't say anything.

"Are you serious?"

The crowds were moving us into the street. I stumbled. "Len, are you sure? How is this possible?"

"That's what I said, how is this possible. I went to see some doctors. I don't want to talk about this. Apparently, I already have."

"How did this start?"

"It started, that's definite."

"Is there a test for Alzheimer's?"

"Short of an autopsy, no."

"Then how do you know?"

He hesitated. "I don't want to get into details, but I got a medical opinion."

"Did you get a second one?"

"I got three."

"God, this is horrible."

"It seems so sudden, doesn't it?"

"Are you sure?"

He didn't reply. I thought of hospitals, people on stretchers with IV drips. I thought of Lenny at his desk. I tried to remember something he did at work that was glitchy, words on his computer screen that were out of order, something he said that was more than a verbal cramp. I couldn't think.

"What did they say about how long it takes?"

Lenny avoided my eyes. "How long it takes to do what?"

I wanted to take that question back. I wanted to go back to where we were a block ago and start over. We started walking more quickly, then slowed down.

"It could be long and slow, Kay. But sometimes it's not. I'm getting a head start. I researched this as much as I could, which might not have been enough. But I got told. There was nothing left to say."

"You've known this for how long?"

"For a while."

"You're gonna leave and not tell anybody?"

"I...I thought about going in to work today and gathering everybody together, the people that are left, and making an announcement. Standing on a chair. But I couldn't. I couldn't. I didn't want to become a spectacle. I didn't want people standing around and watching me do...what? Give a speech? Or watching me go. I didn't want to seem pathetic."

"You're not pathetic! God, just tell me this isn't happening!"

"And there's almost nobody left. They got rid of almost everybody I used to know. As spectacles go, maybe it wouldn't be that bad."

I couldn't think of anything to say. It's like I was the one with a processing glitch.

Lenny cleaned his glasses on his jacket. "I'm trying to think of somebody well-known that has this."

"Somebody famous?"

"Somebody you'd recognize."

Then we were standing around, trying, I guess, to think of somebody famous who had this. I was wracking my brain. My brain fell down and couldn't get up. I thought of how I fell a few blocks ago and Len helped me to my feet. That wasn't what you'd expect somebody with this kind of disease to do but I knew nothing about this disease. Whether I knew anything or not, things just changed. The job just changed. It was like I was going to work in a different place.

"This isn't the way you'd expect this to happen, is it, Kay? Suppose I found out and didn't tell anybody and just came to work as usual."

"So it would have to come out eventually."

"That's the long and short of it, shorty. I could keep it a secret for a while. But I'd start to change. I'd become different while I was still trying to hide it."

"That could still be the scenario if you don't tell anyone but me." I looked around. "Let's go somewhere and talk."

"Then I'd get to where I couldn't hide it. I'd write sentences with the words transposed or the letters mixed up. These are just examples and not good ones, but I can't tell what's next. I'd forget the password for my computer. Then I'd forget two days in a row even though it's on a Post-it note stuck to my computer."

"I forget passwords."

"I'd forget that I forgot."

"How could you forget that you forgot?"

"I'd forget the password to the men's room in the morning, then again when I came back from lunch. Pick a password, I'd forget it. Then I'd forget what a password was. The elevator door would open and I'd forget what to do next. Then I'd have tantrums over nothing. People would start to talk. They'd start to talk *about* me. Then they'd start to talk *to* me. One day I'd walk into the break room and there's everybody with a cake. The cake would be for me. There's the cake and there's the door. We'd eat the cake, then someone would show me the door. It would all be civilized."

"That's not the way this company gets rid of people, is it."

"I decided not to wait for them. I've also had tremors. Thumb tremors. My left thumb."

For a few moments I tried to be in Lenny's head. I was willing to believe part of this, but not all of it.

I was walking ahead of him. Then he was walking ahead of me. Lenny was always the slow poke. *I* walked fast while *he* couldn't keep up. People were careening around us like we weren't there.

"What are you going to do, Len?"

"I'm going to Florida."

"Why?"

"People go there every day."

"Where?"

"The Gulf Coast."

"Now how..."

He stopped walking again. "I'm going to drive down."

"Alone?"

"That's the plan. I'm going to rent a car."

I dug my fingers into my hair which was frizzed out from the humidity. "Len, why are you doing this? You aren't even old enough to retire."

"I'm going to move to an assisted leaving place near St. Petersburg. I had a cousin who grew up there. She checked it out for me. I won't go into all the details, but the staff-to-resident ratio isn't bad. The Medicaid rating is decent."

"Have you ever been to this place, Len?"

He didn't answer. "They say it's better to move somebody with this disease when it's early, while they still have their mental faculties. If you wait too long, the move is more difficult."

"Who said that?"

"The people giving me advice about my mother."

"Why her?"

"For one thing she's 93. For another I thought she might have Alzheimer's. They said she doesn't."

"You're not even 60."

"58."

"Did you get a second opinion?"

"Stop asking me about second opinions!"

"The time isn't right, Len! You seem perfectly healthy! God, what's wrong with you?"

We stopped beside a trash can. "No, the time is right. When I, quote, lose my faculties, unquote, I'll be accustomed to the lifestyle."

"What lifestyle?"

"What I find at the other end."

"This is nutty, Len. Who put you up to this?"

"Nobody. I can't remember when this started, but it started. I'd find myself awake at night and the words in my head sounded weird. A sentence would go by like a runaway train, go off the rails, crash. I'd write it down and it wouldn't make any sense. It was disconcerting, you'll have to take my word for it. I'm not a hypochondriac. I'm not looking for trouble."

"What's this place called?"

Lenny paused. "It's...cheap. There's a bus. Once I'm there, I won't have a car. I'm going to have hundreds of books, though. All the books I've always wanted to read but never did. Books with thin spines, books with thick spines. Books that are perfect-bound and books with sewn bindings. Paperbacks. Books with jackets. Big clunky books and tidy, slender books that are like a ballerina. Oh. You want the name of this place."

He got a piece of paper out of his jacket and read the name. I wasn't listening. Lenny didn't have a partner or spouse. He never got married. He had no kids, no siblings, his brother was dead, he lived alone. He had a dog. *Don't ask about the dog,* I thought. For a moment I thought about myself. Did I have cognitive glitches without knowing it, lying in bed at night, staring at the ceiling? Would I know the difference between a brain cramp and age-related impairment?

I waved the thought away with both hands, like flies buzzing my face. We were hanging on this street corner like a truck might roll up and take it away.

"How'd you manage to swing this, Len?"

"The financing? I'm swinging it, let's put it that way. The funny thing is, I haven't really gone anywhere or spent money on anything in years. I've been saving up for this without really knowing it. Soon I'll start the sprint to Social Security."

"What are you going to do after you get there?"

"Eventually, years from now, I hope I can sit in a wheel chair by the beach and watch the waves."

"What in the world are you talking about? How are you gonna get there?"

"To the rental car place? I'm walking."

"Right now?"

"Any minute."

"How are you gonna get to the beach?"

"I know how I'm getting to Florida. That's all I know. There's a rental car place near Battery Park City. I'm taking my time getting there. There's no deadlines, no stories to edit."

We were still standing around. There was something about the way we were not moving that made me hope he'd change his mind, that there was a second chance. He described the rental car place like he was giving me directions, like it was me going there.

"So where's your luggage?"

"I got rid of most of my stuff," he said. "I sent the essentials down."

"Is it such a good idea to go alone?"

"I could go alone or...what would the opposite of going alone be?"

I clasped my shoulders with my hands. I was hugging myself. I thought about what he was doing when I first saw him on the street.

"I have to confess, Lenny, that I saw you going

through a trash can. Maybe there's a clue there."

"You saw me going through a trash can?"

"After I got out of the subway. I was just walking along and there you were, going through the trash before we met."

"And you stood there and watched while I was going through a trash can?"

"It was an accident."

"That doesn't sound like an accident."

"It was totally accidental."

"Well, me looking in the trash can *wasn't* an accident. And at the time I was in total, full possession of my mental faculties. Quote, unquote."

When I didn't say anything, he said, "This isn't new. I've been looking in trash cans since I was five years old. If it was a big trash can, my brother would lift me up so I could see in."

I didn't say anything. I didn't want to bring up his brother. It wouldn't be a good distraction.

"Wouldn't that be funny, Kay, if one of my last acts as I get out of town was being stalked by a beautiful woman?"

"Who?"

"You."

I scratched my head. "I wasn't stalking you."

"That didn't come out the way I meant it."

"Oh."

"I should say that I've been the stalker myself, rather than the stalkee."

"Who'd you stalk?"

"I have a history of going through trash cans."

"Which ones?"

"I had a history of stalking little girls when I was a little boy."

"Which ones?"

"That came out wrong. I didn't stalk them—I would never do that. I stalked their trash. There was a girl I was in love with in the fifth grade. I used to wait outside her house for her father to take out the trash so I could see if she opened my letters. Or threw them away. If they weren't there, that meant she kept them. If she threw them away opened, at least she might have read them. I never found one unopened. Not that I can remember. That was at least something."

"What happened to her?"

"She's gone."

"Did you keep the letters?"

"For a while, but I let them get away. I kept a lot of junk instead. And my old records are gone. I still have an almost new turntable with Harman Kardon speakers and nothing to play on them. I woke up last night thinking of that Velvet Underground song, `It Takes a Village to Raise a Child.'"

"I'm sorry?"

"`It Takes a Village To Raise a Child.' It was a song by the Velvet Underground."

"I don't think so, Len."

"It was the Velvet Underground. It was the first track on their eponymous first album. I guess they were a little before your time."

"Len, that was the name of a book. Written by a politician. A woman, I think. I can't remember her name, though. Wait—it was a president's wife. Laura Bush, maybe? Or Barbara Bush?"

"No! It was a song! `It Takes a Village to Raise a Child!' The Velvet Underground!"

"It's a book, Len, not a song."

"And it wasn't written by Lou Reed! It was written by Maureen Tucker!"

"She didn't write for them."

"No! It was Maureen! She wrote `It Takes A Village to Raise a Child!'"

He was screaming and his screams were turning heads. I was getting Lou Reed confused with Maureen Tucker and Maureen Tucker with Laura Bush while Lenny was getting really mad. I put my arm around his shoulder because I wanted to calm him. "I think you're mistaken, Lenny. Maureen didn't write songs. She played the drums. Even I know that."

"What the hell do you know about it! It was before your time!"

Lenny stalked down Broadway in a huff. He walked quickly, like he was about to break into a run.

"Len, this is too sudden. Maybe you should take the day off."

"No," he said over his shoulder, "I'm gonna write my own song. It's called `It Takes a Village to Bury This Old Bastard.' That's why I'm moving to this place in Tampa. There's a boardwalk near the ocean, I can take a walk on the boardwalk. I don't care if they're only in it for the money. They got a good staff-to-resident ratio. It's like a village. Don't you get it?"

"No, I don't. You don't have to go there to write that song or any other."

He stopped. I tried to put my arm around him again. He moved away, my hand fell from his shoulder. I walked behind him. People walked in front of me, a whole bunch of them and got between us.

I imagined Lenny in a wheelchair, alone on a beach, not ten years from now but ten months. The tide would slowly rise. The wheels would be stuck in the sand. The sand would turn to mud. The sun would be going down. The wheelchair would start to rock back and forth with the tide. He'd fall out of it. The tide would wash him out to sea. There was no life guard. No sand castles. No place to get lemonade or soft ice cream. I was hugging myself. I wanted to cry. I wanted to be there, to pull him out of the water, to call for help. I was nowhere to be found. Where was I? I was back on Broadway, where it was still dark.

"Len, how about this. Let's go to the office. We'll pretend we didn't meet this way, but then we'll meet after work. Maybe you've had medical opinions, but you need to talk to a friend, too. I think this is too sudden. I hope you didn't give notice."

I waited for an answer but kept walking. A wave of people came behind us who looked like they were moving down from the Occupy Wall Street site. Placards were bobbing over their heads. Bystanders had to back out of the way. It took a few minutes for them to pass by. When they were gone, I noticed that the person I was talking to wasn't Lenny.

"Lenny?"

Whoever it was gave me an incredulous look— not unlike Lenny—but kept on going and disappeared. It wasn't Len. I looked around. Where did he go? He wasn't there.

I shouted, *Len? Len?* Nobody answered. Lenny wasn't there. One minute he was standing next to me, the next he was gone like he was never there. It was like he got swept away, swallowed up by the crowd.

And then I was alone on Broadway. The crowd thinned out. While we were talking, I found my company badge hanging from my neck. I brought it after all. I could get in the building without him.

Chapter Six

I walked the streets off Lower Broadway looking for Lenny. I did it calmly but couldn't find the car rental place. The more I looked, the more futile it seemed. I was getting lost.

I stopped in the middle of a block. It was the one with the building I worked in, but I was standing at the back and didn't recognize it at first. I went in.

The 22nd floor was deserted. There was a smear of light from the windows facing the water. The elevator bank was in the middle of the floor, surrounded by a thousand square feet of ratty green carpet. Across from the elevators was a receptionist module. It was piled with boxes after they got rid of the receptionists. The floor was chopped up into hundreds of low-rise cubicles, arrayed in haphazard sections with glass-walled offices here and there.

Lenny didn't mention a meeting with human resources. He said nothing about being forced out. He never mentioned his 93-year-old mother *not* having Alzheimer's but he said he had it himself, even though he was still in his 50s. How typical was this? I compared him to my parents, who were separated and died young during the same month. My sister and I buried them in Montana. We were too old to be orphans but that's what it felt like. We weren't close to them. It's something I don't like to think about. We each inherited $321.

I turned on some lights on the way to my chair. There were no cubicles where we sat, just a long U-shaped counter top that worked its way around a rectangular area about the size of a one-bedroom apartment. Because it was all like one big desk, it wasn't really clear where one reporter's space ended and the next one began. The elbow of the reporter next to you could be a foot from your face. Once there was constant noise from people talking on the phone.

That's the way it was when we had 20 reporters. There were four left. There was more "space" but if the person that sat next to you left, it felt like there was a void instead of more space. I was at one end of the U, Lenny sat all the way around at the opposite end, so our backs were to each other. I had to turn all the way around to talk to him unless I rolled my chair next to his.

His space was the biggest. There was a drawer that hung from his desk, like a tab at the end of a file folder, with his computer keyboard. The name plate over his desk said *Editor in Chief* and was made of metal. Everybody else had a plastic sign.

The managing editor and all the other editors were gone. The freelancer who started last winter still came in three days a week to try and cover for the people that left. The copy desk was on another floor— we shared it with six other publications. We used to have our own. Above where I sat was a red, black and white sign with a picture of Jesus that said:

SINners Repent!

A managing editor hung it and left it there after he got fired. We sent him a million e-mails, asking when he was going to take this away. He claimed that he wasn't allowed back in the building. I've become inured to what goes on here, but I was really tired of looking at this thing. I wrote memos to facilities asking that they do *something* with it. A guy came by to polish it.

Once 80 people worked here, when we had a real newsroom in a different part of town. We'd made six moves in the last five years, each one to a smaller space. *SIN* once had a conference business. There were dozens of people who sold ads back when it was all words on paper. A dozen more who sold subscriptions on the phone when 50 issues cost $898 a year. There was a big fight before they decided to cut back to 40 times a year without lowering the price. Then we went free, like a million other trade papers. People left. We started to disappear.

Where did all those people go? Where did all the money go? It was the money that went first, then the people. Or the people, then the money, then more people. I was writing more for the web. I wouldn't know if they could make as much money selling ads on the web as in the newspaper. I have no idea what it's like to sell ads. There were going to be fewer people here no matter what.

The website never got a formal rollout. It just appeared. The people working on it were on another floor. Not all of the stories in the paper showed up on the website. Some were on the website that never made the paper.

The web stories were shorter than the ones in the newspaper. They'd start as a Word file, Len would get them, then the webheads. The copy desk might look at them. The next time I saw them they were back on my computer screen when I looked at the website. There was never that cut to paper and I never printed hard copies of the web stories. I always picked up errors on paper that I missed on the screen.

People could post anonymous comments about my web stories, impugn my integrity, call me names and vanish. Or they could point out glaring errors that would be seen by the industry. Other newspapers had gone full digital. Readers' comments to their stories were often a lot more interesting than the stories themselves.

More importantly, management could see how many people were reading what I wrote. Someday I could be called into an office and told, "Kay, you're not click bait. When can you make yourself more attractive to our audience?" I can feel it getting closer. I'd get an email, not facetime.

We used to have editorial meetings on Monday morning to plan the week's issue. That gradually ended. Lenny started meeting with you individually. Then the meetings stopped. He'd say something to you in the break room or the elevator. As people left and weren't replaced, you'd think there'd be more time for that but it happened less. When Lenny met with web services, I wasn't included. He didn't exactly refuse to discuss those meetings but he was cagey.

I avoided all this to a fault. I should have been pissed off that changes were being made in secret. I should have demanded to know what was going on. At some point I was afraid of what I might hear.

There was a cardboard box by Lenny's chair. When you got fired or laid-off, somebody from facilities dropped one off. You filled it with your stuff and they shipped it to you later. Len had been here for decades. For him they'd need a dumpster.

It was empty, but he had one, so HR must know he's gone. They must have a forwarding address. They'd never give it to me.

I sat at my desk and tried to reach him. His home phone was disconnected. If he was on his way to Florida he didn't live there anymore. Like me, Lenny was one of these nuts with no mobile device.

I had a list of people we both worked with. Let's say he hadn't told anybody he was leaving. Do I want to be the one to break the news? Once people heard, they'd think SIN was unraveling like a cheap sweater. They'd keep their distance. My phone wouldn't ring as much. There'd be fewer e-mails. Even if I did nothing, the word would get out. The more I thought about it, the less interest I had in answering questions about Lenny. I had enough of my own.

I thought of getting up and turning on more lights. Instead I sat in the dark. I was hungry, I'd had no breakfast. I didn't feel like hunting for take-out.

I typed Alzheimer's into a search window but didn't press return. I imagined being taken to a website and finding Lenny's picture. Or a podcast with Lenny's last words.

I didn't see any of this coming. I saw him on Saturday. If I'd said hello, the Alzheimer's reveal might have come out. What would that have been like? Since I hadn't filed the multi-asset class trading piece, we would have talked about that instead. That would have been a distraction. The story went into a section of the paper that supported long deadlines. But it was already getting old.

I wanted to go out and have a drink with him— one last act. If I did it Saturday I probably wouldn't have been there when Doris called. We could have said good-bye without watching the clock. We could have gone out for dinner. I knew a place, the Riverrun Café I wanted to try. I don't know what we would have done after that. What would happen to Florida?

I was looking at that empty box. It haunted me, like I was waiting for him to call. I could wait all day and nothing would happen. This was putting me in an awful mood.

The phone rang. The caller ID screen blinked off. "Hello?"

"Is Kay there?"

"Who wants to know?"

"Doris Morris."

"Oh." I grabbed a pen. "Doris, I wasn't expecting you. Kind of early, isn't it?"

"I said I would call, didn't I?"

"Actually, you didn't."

"So Kay...I guess you're wondering why I called you here."

"Why did you?"

There was still no name on the caller ID screen. There was no number. Then there was nothing at the other end of the line.

"Doris? You there?"

"Yeah. I bet you know why I'm calling."

"Why don't you tell me."

"I figured you want to talk about the call center."

"I do."

Doris cleared her throat. I could hear people in the background. "Doris, where are you calling from?"

"Never mind. The call center thing is over. I can't talk about that. Don't call me again."

"Oh?"

Doris took a breath. "I can't talk to you. Ever."

"Why?"

"Everything I told you? I take it back. Don't repeat what I said."

"Don't repeat what?"

"Nobody should know the things I told you, Kay."

"What things?"

"Never mind, Kay."

"What things? And who would care about them?"

"Just skip it."

"Is it any of the people I met?"

"If you see me at the gym, don't talk to me."

"How's Stella? How's her mother?"

"It's not your business."

"Is she getting evicted?"

"It's none of your business."

"What if I see you at the gym?"

"I can't afford to know you or be seen with you."

"Wait a minute, Doris. Let's back up. What about those people I met yesterday?"

"I gotta go."

"Slow down, Doris. If you're worried about how this looks, it's gonna look weird if you pretend you don't know me when there are people who know that we're friends."

"Who?"

"The people at the gym, the people I met from the call center."

"We're not friends, Kay."

"They know we're acquainted. Those two women who attacked you in the shower know we're friends. It's going to look weird."

"I don't care how it looks. I'm not gonna be somebody's source or witness for some *story*."

"We never said you'd be identified. But that doesn't mean we can't talk later or make a different arrangement."

"There's no arrangement. I disappeared, ok? We never even met."

"You only called me a million times, Doris. Fedloan has a record of those calls."

"Those records get destroyed."

"Doris—I've got voicemail messages from you

and the number you called from at Fedloan. You sent me emails. They're not like letters you can throw in the trash. E-mails are forever."

There was silence on the other end. I was trying to think of a way to pivot from a situation she found threatening. If only I hadn't answered the phone. But there was no guarantee that she'd leave a message.

There was a sigh, then another. "I'm just the messenger here, Kay. Stella doesn't want me hanging out with you because of what I said about her and my father. I promised I wouldn't tell anybody about that and I did. First my old man does something bad to her, now I did something too. That all stops right here, right now."

"Fine, I won't put it in the story."

"Stella says how do you leave it out? I'm thinking the same thing."

"Easy. I won't write it."

"You say you won't write it but how do we know? Somebody you're writing this for could say put that chick Stella in the story."

"I won't mention Stella."

"You're sayin that now but what about later?"

"Give me a number for that supervisor guy at the call center who you said was fed up and we'll say we're done for now. But I wanna talk to Stella and reassure her."

"Stay away from Stella. I told you too much about her."

"How's your father, Doris?"

The line went dead.

A phone number came up on the caller ID screen. I didn't see it at first because it was so faint. My pen skipped, then flew through the air while I looked for something else to write with. I found a pencil just as the number blinked off the screen. 609-867-5---. I didn't get the last three digits. How many combinations would I have to try before I got the right number? Unless I went to a phone booth, she would know it was me if I called back. If she didn't answer, I'd still be left hanging.

You couldn't retrieve a record of calls from the phone on my desk. The phones here needed an upgrade. So did my chair. The lever you raised and lowered it with wasn't working. I thought about the chair Doris sat in at the call center. The same chair that she complained about and didn't sit in anymore.

I tapped out an e-mail to the telecom people. *Hi, I need a number from area code 609 that called at 7:10 AM. Could you find it for me? Thanks, Kay P.*

After I hit send, I remembered that the telecom people sometimes didn't get here until noon. If it was a number in New Jersey, Doris wouldn't be there long. It could be Stella's mother's number. If she got evicted, it would be disconnected. Probably. I shouldn't have asked about her father. What was I thinking?

I opened my drawer. The phone number Doris gave me when we were drinking on Saturday night was there. I dialed it up. There was nothing on the other end.

When I got up this morning, I thought I might have a story which would lead to another, then another. It was in pieces all over my apartment. There were things I'd never think of that the call center posse probably saw every day. They gave me a start, but just a start. I needed at least somebody to put their name to this.

Stella would be out. I didn't know about the others and I couldn't reach them. Doris was still my only hope. She'd never give up her father. That would mean giving up Stella. But she already did.

Suppose the new news website balked when they saw what I had so far. What would another editor say to this, pitched by an unheralded and maybe unemployed freelancer who appeared from cyberspace? "So Kay, you've got five people and they all worked at the same call center. But you only know how to contact one of them? And she's off the record? I don't know, Kay, I don't know..."

My foot would be in the door, but only one of them. The trick would be to find an editor who knew higher ed finance. I was starting from scratch on that, too.

There are reporters who would get a call like this and say, "Wow, I *must* be on to something. Never mind that Doris told the posse not to talk to me. Never mind how crazy this was while a lot of what she was telling me might not be true—this is a good get!"

If she changed gyms, I'd never see her there. She'd be on the move if the payday loan caught up with her. Suppose she was sitting with the posse in the Crown Vic and described our walk on the Boardwalk. Stella'd say, "You told that chick Kay about what you did with the payday loan? Oh my god! She's gonna write about that! If the law sees it, you'll go to jail!" It could end just like that.

Doris and Stella could be a couple. Or they could have been on verge of being one or about to break up. Or not be a couple at all. If Doris was gone, I didn't know if I could start nearly from scratch and still turn out 5000 words a week about trading technology and government regulation. Especially with no Lenny. *SIN* could disappear just like Lenny and Doris.

That's what life was like here. People left. Publications that had been around for decades just disappeared. I got Doris's photo of herself up on my screen. Her smile seemed smaller. She was looking less and less like somebody I knew. I could track down Destiny Childs, their co-worker Doris described who got behind on her student loan at a for-profit college. She didn't work at Fedloan anymore. Maybe she'd talk.

I'm stubborn. I was sold on this story. But I started to give up. Plus I left my notebook in Stella's freakin car.

I went over to Lenny's desk. It would have made more sense if he'd left on Friday. I only knew about this because I bumped into him on his way out of town. But he *did* leave the newspaper on Friday. Everything was where he left it.

There was the same crud you'd find on anyone's desk. A leg that raised his keyboard was missing and replaced by a paper weight that said *Greetings from Green Bay!* Len grew up in Wisconsin. Then there were stacks of newspapers and every other kind of paper, legal size, letter size, reams of it, sliding into the space next to him where somebody used to sit.

Near the keyboard was a single sheet of paper. It was a letter that began:

> *Dear Kay Pigeon:*
> *You want to...*

He was writing in long hand. He got three words into it. Six counting the salutation. I sat in his chair trying to imagine what he was going to say next and why he stopped there. I just saw him. What did he have to tell me that he couldn't say out loud? What did he think I wanted?

There were packets of mustard. Broken pencils.

Paper clips. Thumb drives, rubber bands, band aids. I wanted to scoop them up and put them somewhere.

There was a framed picture of a young woman in a purplish tie-dyed blouse. It was Chloe Macchiaroli, Len's old flame. They both worked here three decades ago. She left a few years after he started.

Len's space made me think of the display window of a toy store in a small town, like the one where he grew up. There was an Erector Set box. A box of Lincoln Logs. The Post-It notes on his computer screen overlapped like bark on a tree. Near it were four statuettes with big heads out of proportion to their plastic bodies. Captain Kangaroo and George Washington. Jonathan Winters and Babe Ruth. They all looked alike, especially Jonathan Winters and Babe Ruth, like they came from the same bobblehead doll factory. They predated bobblehead dolls. There were adult men who were obsessed with bobbleheads. If you asked any of them "So you're into dolls?" the response wouldn't be uplifting.

Behind them were three lady puppets about three feet tall, circus-like figures with garish makeup. Each stood on a pedestal that went up their dresses. Their hair looked fake but felt real. They appeared last winter.

The longer they were there, the weirder they seemed. The more Len explained their significance, the more mysterious they became. His father's family brought them from Europe and in the 1850s went west in a covered wagon. The puppets were hundreds of years old and were thought to be inhabited by supernatural forces that were aligned with God but behaved like a poltergeist. They helped move the covered wagon across the prairie to a strange land— Nebraska wasn't a state yet. The wagon stopped rolling when the animals pulling it died. The poltergeist disappeared like the snow in the spring. That was the story that was handed down.

A hundred years later Lenny was a small child in Wisconsin who became obsessed with these puppets he found in the attic. When other kids slept with their footballs and Tonka toys, he took these painted puppets to bed with him. They were life-like, not anatomically, but in their faces. They were like painted ladies of yore. Innocent looking but jaded.

One weekend when we were working late, he described sneaking into the attic and bringing the puppets to bed with him. He tried to take their clothes off and couldn't, so he took off his pajamas. This went on for most of the second grade, when his mother and father discovered him one night, naked in bed with the puppets.

His parents belonged to a Protestant sect that was as malevolent as it was obscure. His mother had relatives who were connected to the Salem witch trials in Massachusetts. They tied Lenny to the bed. They prayed to Jesus for guidance. They untied him. They tied him up again the next night. The next day when he came home from school, they made him sit at the dining room table and begin to copy in long hand the Old Testament from Gideon's Bible, the one you'd find in a hotel room. The spirit that inhabited the puppets was back, his father said, or never left. His parents decided that he had to seek forgiveness and do penance to prove that he was worthy for reasons that were never explained. It was unclear how long it would take. His brother was sent away to live with relatives.

Every day after school he scratched out page after page on a Big Chief writing tablet. The puppets stood watch over him, to remind him of why he was there. His parents feared God's wrath because of what he'd done with the puppets, warning him not to tell anyone. It went on the next day and the day after that and the day after that—every day except Sunday but sometimes into the night. Len thought that God was omnipresent then, but he was also never really there. Was there a god, that was the question.

He didn't read well enough to know what he was writing. He copied letters by rote, like a child monk in a monastery. There was no let up. When he cried for relief, his father beat him. The beatings were ritualistic. They did things to him that they'd go to jail for today— that's the story Len told. The puppets remained at the dining room table. By the fourth grade, 170 Big Chief tablets were piled in the basement, filled with pages from the Old Testament. It stopped that year when his father was hit by a truck on a road behind their house.

Len went into the Air Force when he was 17. He wanted to fly away, literally. I've been around people in the military—my father and his buddies—and Len didn't seem like the type at all. He broke out photos of himself in uniform.

He didn't fly. He was shipped to Malmstrom Air Force Base in Montana and was buried in a Minuteman ICBM missile launch control center where people were known as missileers. Lenny insisted that if Montana was a separate country, it would have the fourth largest nuclear weapons force in the world, with hundreds of missiles lurking in underground silos. He was cagey about what happened there, but said he was around people who had the launch codes.

Richard Nixon was President. It was around the time of Watergate. There was talk of impeachment and stories that Nixon was drunk in the White House. Could an inebriated or unstable President with the nuclear football and the Gold Codes start an unprovoked nuclear war? Len thought it could fall to the operations people to ultimately make that decision. They were the last mile.

I didn't challenge him on this. At the time I didn't know him that well, but just well enough to figure that he hated the Air Force. I know I would have.

Len would say, "I don't have a nuclear war story to tell because there was no nuclear war." He wanted to fly, not be assigned to Malmstrom. Then he didn't want to fly anymore. He wanted out.

I thought of what he said about crazed COBOL programmers when we were on the street. He studied COBOL in the Air Force, an early computer language. Did he forget? They sent him to code school at Vandenberg Air Force Base in California. He made writing COBOL code sound like copying the Old Testament into Big Chief writing tablets. He had a nervous breakdown and ended up in a hospital. The Cold War was still on when he was discharged and moved to the Virgin Islands where he got his first newspaper job. I don't know how long he stayed. There are gaps in his life I know nothing about.

I picked up the picture of Chloe. She looked like she was in love. I wondered who took the photo. Lenny started in the mailroom but with Chloe's help, talked his way into a reporter job. They sat next to each other in the newsroom and became a couple, living in the same building but not in the same apartment. Then she left for a newspaper in South America. Her mother lived in Venezuela and was sick. Chloe said it was temporary and that she'd return soon.

He waited. Her picture remained but Chloe never

came back. Decades later, the puppets returned instead.

They appeared last winter after his mother sold their house and he returned home to fetch some mementos. I looked at them and thought: this is what he wanted to save? He was gloomy, even for him, the day that the puppets appeared on his desk. I tried to be light. "Len," I said, "why bring these dolls here—excuse me, puppets? I don't think Jonathan Winters is getting lonely." "Actually, it's me," he said. I asked what was making him lonely. He waved me away.

Puppets, dolls and indescribable junk piled up. His desk became an eyesore. People walking by would stop and stare. Management let it go. He kept the newspaper together when it was making money. By then it was the job that ate his life, not the job that ate his brain.

For a while I thought, ok, he's got these puppets on his desk. This is pretty benign. Then I thought, no, maybe this was like a cry for help that came too late. I'd watch him and the puppets out of the corner of my eye. He'd look at Chloe's photo. He'd look at the puppets. He'd look at Chloe's photo. She'd be over 50 now. If they passed each other on the street, he might not recognize her. He recognized the puppets, though.

There was a pink window envelope at the edge of his desk. It was addressed to human resources with my name on it. I read the address three times. The words were blurry until they came into focus. It was a letter from a debt collection agency. They were going after me because of the Grad PLUS Loans. The student loan situation was bad enough when I left on Saturday. Today I was in default.

I almost smacked one of the puppets. This *had* to be a mistake. Fedloan, the loan servicer, had not notified me about this. This could *not* be right. I got up, walked around, and sat at Len's desk again.

Why did Lenny get this? The HR person who opened it probably didn't know me but knew Len. I started to panic. I thought about how hopeful we were when Leenie left for the west coast. She kept saying, "Wait till I get my own place, Mom. You can visit me." I wondered when she stopped saying that. I couldn't stay with her where she was living now. There was no room. There was no hotel. The word was don't bother to visit at all.

I was looking for the button to Lenny's desk lamp when some lights went on at the other end of the floor. More lights came on. Brian Dickey appeared.

"Hey Kay, what are you doing here so early?"

I was startled. "Oh, Brian. Hi. I could ask you the same question."

"Ask away. What's up?"

He walked over and stood next to me. I was frantically trying to appear like I wasn't sitting at Len's desk. I shoved the collection agency letter under a pile of papers. He didn't seem to notice.

He tapped me on the shoulder. "In case you didn't know, Lenny's left us."

"Really?"

"Yup. He's gone."

He didn't notice the letter Len was writing to me and made no remark about where I was sitting.

"You should have gotten an e-mail about SEO," Brian said. "Let's discuss it."

There was no discussion. He left. I thought I'd better move back to my own desk. I thought about the time and how early it was.

Brian was VP of business development, probably in his mid-20s, blond hair, bigger than me. He often seemed to talk faster than he could think and had a one-year MBA. He appeared taught and controlled. He seemed unruly and undisciplined just as often.

Every day he wore the same pull-overs I wore, almost exactly the same, to the point where I thought of buying new ones. They plunged slightly at the neckline, just enough to reveal that he wasn't wearing a tie. Men in this place still wore ties but word was they were on the way out. Brian was pushing the envelope. Or losing his tie.

After he came here and we were introduced, he started calling me Bird Girl. "That's not my name," I said. "Call me Kay." "Kay?" he said. "That's a real boring name." "No more boring than Brian," I replied. "It's Kay. K-a-y."

I couldn't tell if he was being an asshole or trying to be cute. He wasn't the first. The bio in my high school year book said:

KAY PIGEON = BIRDGIRL.

My second brother-in-law—the brother of my second husband—thought my name was a practical joke. "Kay Pigeon? Kay *Pigeon*? I'm going to start calling you *Clay* Pigeon after my bro shoots you down." Clay pigeons are what skeet shooters—like this brother-in-law—shoot at when they did target practice with their long rifles. That family loved their guns. They not only had guns in their trucks, but under their beds, under their pillows, a thousand miles from where Brian was standing.

My bro-in-law was off by six months when he

predicted when we'd split up, even if neither of us predicted the reason. No one objected when I took the kids. It was a pyrrhic victory but at least I won on. I never changed my name when I got married. Other people had already been doing it for me with this tricked-out nick name. It didn't stop with Bird Girl. In college it was Bird Woman but very often Bird Person which I preferred to the first two.

Actually, I don't like any of them. Some people think calling me *Bird* is clever. Trying to convince them that it's not is often more trouble than it's was worth. Some people find me threatening. If calling me *Bird* makes them feel less threatened—it's fine, unless I decide it's not.

I don't know how Brian got here. He was from Palm Beach. I don't think many people from South Florida turn up on Wall Street, although Palm Beach probably isn't South Florida—I'm not sure. His degree was from a private college in the east, I'm blanking on the one, maybe one of the women's colleges that now admit men. Brian was cloaked in privilege, even if the fit wasn't always snug.

Brian talked about outcomes. Ending up in a place like this might not lead to a great outcome if he couldn't leave for something better. The fact that he was VP of business development when a lot of his friends were unemployed wouldn't be enough. I was clueless about what somebody with his job title did. That's because I don't know much about the publishing side, the business side of this business. For some reason, I'm not real curious about the company I work for. I stick to my knitting.

But he was playing a role in editorial. That's not so unusual, but it extended to telling us *how* to write, not just *what* to write. First it was subtle. Then there were dumb questions. Whether they were dumb or not wasn't the thing. The fact that *he* was asking them worried me.

I didn't know what time he normally got here. It didn't matter. We were here. The day had started. I didn't see him at the meeting on Saturday upstairs with the hedge fund people.

Brian and Lenny were a match made in hell. Lenny used to run interference between editorial and the publishing side. I assumed he would be a buffer between Brian and the reporters that were still here. But people weren't paying attention to Lenny like they used to. And he wasn't here.

I looked up and Brian was there. "You read the message, Kay?"

"About?"

"SEO."

"What's SEO?"

He looked at me like I was his hopeless little sister. No, his hopeless mother.

"It's search engine optimization, Kay. Read the message. I'll be right back. Don't go away."

As soon as he turned the corner I looked at the collection agency letter. I was furious again. Why didn't I hear from the loan servicer? Why didn't Lenny tell me about this? I picked it up and took it over to my desk. The letter looked legitimate. I didn't want to sit there with this thing on my desk. I went back and sat in Lenny's chair.

It was 2011, the start of a new decade. I started to think ahead to a year from now. A decade from now. To a time when SEO became like the ENTER key on your keyboard until it was replaced by something else. Lots of things we were going to talk about would eventually be gone. Even if nothing was gone, would I still be able to get a job? If this job ended, how long would I have to wander the dark corridors of the internet before I found someone who'd pay me a salary I could live on to write words no one had to pay to read? How long would that be the status quo?

I knew what SEO was, sort of. For us it means how we draw eyeballs to our website and keep them there. I wasn't sure if it was still considered new or in some nether region between new and not new. The surprise was that it took this long for somebody to say *here's our SEO strategy, fit in.* It was just a question of who would deliver the message. It wasn't a good sign that I didn't know it could be Brian.

I tried to read between the lines of Lenny's letter but there was only one. I was still at his desk when Brian came back.

"Are you ready?" he said. "You don't look like you're ready."

"What am I ready for?"

"So what's going to happen is you'll get a word list. You showed initiative by getting here early, so you get a heads up. Use the list for your headlines."

"I don't write headlines. The copy desk does."

"Not any more—now you do it. Really, Kay, you've been at this long enough so that writing some headlines shouldn't be a stretch. Or do some copy-editing in case something happens to the copy desk."

"Like what?"

"Nothing yet, but there's this question of how much we need copy editors. Or how many."

"Did Len see this?"

"Lenny doesn't work here anymore. Remember?"

"I'm remembering."

"If Lenny were here, he'd say suck it up, wouldn't

he, Kay?"

"Lenny would never say *suck it up.*"

"This will help you do your job better."

"I doubt it."

"It's going to make you *purr.*"

"It's going to make me suck. All I do is stare at websites all day. It's making me withdrawn."

"You're whining, Kay. That's not gonna expand the enterprise."

"Our stories don't go viral, Brian. We're in a narrow vertical. We don't write about the Kardashians."

Brian's mouth curved into a smile. I was mainly on the phone pestering sources, not on the web. But more and more people wanted an e-mail, not a phone call. A lot of them sent me to their websites. Sometimes there was nobody here but me and the only voice you heard was mine.

I thought of Lenny on a beach in a wheel chair. I thought of him alone in a room behind a locked door. The assisted living place that he thought was going to be ok could become more like a jail. I thought of him screaming for someone to come get him, to let him out.

Then I thought about what I just said to Brian and the way those words were left hanging. I coughed. "My concern, Brian, is with being a team player. I want to be on the team."

"Good. This is like finding out what position you'll play."

"I'm not trying to pick a fight with you."

"Cool. We'll flow in the same river together."

I imagined the clock in my bedroom where the numbers were turning over. The numbers were blurry. I was weary. I couldn't bring myself to say that I just didn't want to talk right now because if I did, I'd have to tell Brian why—and I'd still have to talk to him. I had no good excuses at my fingertips. I'm bad at lying.

"When is SEO going to happen, Brian? Will it be phased in? A Big Bang?"

He became tentative. "So I think there will be algorithms."

"Who's writing them?"

"I don't think those algos have been written yet."

"Are they going to lead to machine-made stories."

He pointed to my computer. "You already have a machine."

"This machine doesn't write."

"Exactly. You pick the words. A person decides. Just like a person will code up the algorithms. See? It's all about people."

"Are algos, or algo-like facsimiles, going to be used to write my stories?"

"So that will never happen."

"It will happen if there's a demand for it."

Brian was looking into the distance, at a place just over my shoulder. He swallowed. He swallowed again. I imagined that my words were stuck in his craw. They weren't going down well. I imagined joining that legion of contract workers working from home, mostly without a contract or with one that was really onerous. The person I'd end up working for would probably be Brian or someone like him. He would Skype his way into my life, onto the laptop in my bedroom and in my face.

Brian moved slightly to my left. He was turning red. It was like he stepped on a button and his face swelled up.

"Kay, let me explain a few *facts*, since you newspaper guys try to deal in *facts*. First, you sound disgruntled about your role. Personally? I'm not paid to worry about the future of journalism as far as the content goes—or these people who think they can just pound out words for a living and that's all they ever do. Words are commoditized, everybody uses them. Anybody can write them. What I *care* about is making *money* in this *business!* I *care deeply* about the *ads* and the *traffic* on my website! Words are everywhere, money is harder to come by!"

Brian picked up a copy of *The New York Times* from the space next to Lenny's desk. "So here's your typical news website, this is their home page."

"That's made out of paper."

"Paper or plastic, it's still their home page, their landing page, their internet presence."

He flipped it over and pointed to a banner ad on the front page below the fold. "See this? This is what matters. They can have their masthead or whatever it's called, they can have their bylines and their stories and their words as long as they leverage SEO. It's all cool as long as I get my ads, page views and clicks. So things are being revolutionized. I get that this is threatening to some people but in the long run, you'll be empowered to do things you never could before!"

Brian smiled. "Although now we can see how many people are reading your stories and whether or not you're click bait. Are you click bait, Kay? Can you go from click bait to being a social media hero?"

A facilities guy came by pushing a trash can on wheels with broom handles sticking out of the top. He stopped to pick up some trash. A tantrum my son had when he was four came back to me. I tried to coax him to end the screaming meemies by telling me what was wrong. "Use your words, Roddie," I said soothingly, "use your words." I was going to have to use my words.

Brian waited until the facilities guy went around a corner. He started talking very quickly.

"So everything in tech and media is going to be constantly refreshed, renewed. Think of the *refresh* button on your computer. Learn to love that concept. But we're also now in this universe of unpaid content. So through ad buys, branded content, sponsored content, reprint sales and the like, we're trying to get people to *pay* for what we do here when they might get it *free* somewhere else, even in a niche market like ours."

His tone changed. "What keeps me awake at night is that there's content out there that's mostly available for free or cheap which I think is better than our content we're trying to sell ads for, even though I admittedly don't know our space yet. Are you up for this?"

"I got up too early. I admit it."

"That's not what I mean."

Dust flew from the stack of newspapers by Lenny's desk as Brian threw a copy of the *Times* on top of it. He folded his arms. He pulled out his phone. His phone was like another person who pulled up a chair and sat down, but one only he could talk to. He began tapping it with his finger.

Lenny had old copies of *SIN* going back 20 years. The current version was tabloid-sized and had a certain charm. It had the crashing type face of a 1940s tab with serifs and dingbats everywhere. Here was an old-fashioned newspaper that covered digital technology. The people who wrote for it were experienced, knowledgeable reporters. The brain trust upstairs didn't know what to do with it and were running it into the ground. Meanwhile there were a million new news websites that seemed to come from nowhere. Who could trust what they had to say? I could see myself being buried by things I couldn't feel or touch while I was a captive to something that could disappear.

Fifty years ago, I could have been an apprentice in the composing room of a newspaper scrunched behind a Linotype machine, churning out hot type amid crashing metal parts set in motion by a keyboard. I'd heard that at some newspapers, Linotype operators were the editors of last resort. If they found spelling errors, they fixed them. If they didn't like what you wrote, they changed it. They probably wouldn't hire me because I'm a woman. Or I'd have to give my supervisor a blow job to get a try out. It'd be the Go Go 1960s, the Sexual Revolution, whatever that was, was getting close. I imagined bending over Lenny's desk while he slipped me the tube steak as they said in my flaming youth.

That's not how he behaved though. He could be tough but was also kind. Even though he was still in love with the long-gone Chloe, I'd seen him with other women. I was never one of them. Even when we became close, Lenny kept his distance. Even though I really liked him, I kept mine. I didn't plan it. I don't know what he planned for. I never asked. It just so happened that nothing ever happened.

If it was him and me in the last century at some newspaper that doesn't exist anymore, would he have hired me? The men who worked there would be up in arms. Things were significantly worse in those days than they are now. That's the conventional wisdom, the one I keep hearing.

Brian looked up from his phone. "What's your cell phone number, Kay?"

"I don't have one."

"Don't have?"

"I don't have a cell phone."

"Why?"

"Nope."

"Why?"

"It's cheaper."

"Kay—how can you not have a cell phone? I can't believe that."

"Believe it. I don't want my life contained on a handheld device that I could lose or somebody could hack."

"Who would want to hack into your life, Kay?"

"A hacker. Or the federal government. Or a data vendor who'd get my data and use it to sell me stuff I don't need. I'm always getting ads on my laptop for penis enlargement therapies. Somebody paid for that. Somebody out there has my data and I don't know who they are or how they got it."

Brian smiled. "Well, as luck would have it, I have to step away for a few minutes. I'll be right back. Don't go away."

He left.

I used the money I saved from not having a cell phone to buy healthier food. I could get lunch somewhere besides a fast-food chain or a food truck. I didn't want to give up the phones in my apartment tethered to a wire going into a wall. There were no worries about the battery or dropped calls.

There was also another benefit. No cell phone let me stay free of my kids. *Stay free* is the wrong way of putting it. It prevented me from meddling, anytime anywhere.

I was young when they were born. Was I more crazed at that age than they ever were? There are things I did back then that have been hard to live down. I've given my heartfelt apologies, but when they ask what went wrong, I never have answers either of them are satisfied with.

I'm left to worry about them, especially Leenie. If I had a cell phone, I'd never stop phoning. I'd be walking down the street wanting to make another call because I'd be obsessing about the last call. A mobile device would let me phone anywhere, any time. Not having one let me leave them alone. I couldn't call them from the street, a restaurant or the bathroom in a restaurant— or send text messages. I like the idea of telephones being in a fixed place. When I call you, I'm either at home or at work. I can't fake you out by saying I'm in one place when I'm really in another and you can't tell because I'm on a mobile phone.

I found myself waiting for Brian. I thought about getting my calculator and running the student loan numbers but didn't. Leenie and Rod were floating away from me as I pictured Lenny on a beach in his wheel chair before he was washed out to sea.

For a moment I could imagine never seeing my kids again. Even if Leenie and I were estranged, there was still that loan. Rod didn't depend on me at all and that put a different kind of distance between us. Some people disown their kids and some kids disown their parents. If Rod became more distant, I wouldn't completely hate it because at least he was doing well. You often can't tell who will and who won't. I worried that he would feel rejected because his father left and that would somehow screw up his adulthood. Broken relationships were the ones he knew best. And Leenie was the favorite.

Instead he got a really good job in finance. Great salary, no student loans, no problems with drugs, no gaming addiction. He was the independent one.

He got married young like I did but his partner seemed solid, competent. I met her. I could tell she didn't like me. When I left the room, she didn't speak to him in a normal tone. She whispered.

They moved to San Francisco. The view from their condo in Pacific Heights was a long way from the Missouri bootheel or the crappy part of Denver. San Francisco wasn't a place where people went to foment rebellion anymore in the way they once did. If you take away the trendy, e-commerce hype and the sops to gender equality and gay rights people there seem pretty conservative. They don't wear it on their sleeve. It takes you by surprise.

He got a job at a bank on the foreign exchange trading desk. By then I was covering forex. Was this an opportunity for us to bond? Not when I was writing stories that were critical of his business. I went from problematic mother to asshole reporter who gave no credit to the really smart people like himself who helped grow the economy. We couldn't see each other clearly for all the baggage that was too heavy to move.

That didn't stop Rod from helping me with the PLUS Loans. That often gets left out of what I recall about the payment history. He only gave me money for one payment and it was hard for me to ask. Maybe it took some effort for him to write the check. I swore I would never take money from my kids. I took the money, even if I only took it once. He mailed me a paper check.

The money stopped the day he called and asked me how it was going. After I made a payment with his money, it posted to the Stafford, not PLUS—like all the payments I'd made myself since Fedloan became the servicer. It was the same thing that had been going on for months. So I had to explain this crazy situation. Stafford was getting paid, PLUS was still delinquent. I had to explain it twice. When I mentioned that the loan balance kept rising, he said, "Oh my god—this is negative amortization! Because you're not covering the interest and fees, your loan balance is going up instead of down! And this loan is from the federal government? This is how my tax dollars are spent?"

A screaming argument followed. I reminded him that the money was for Leenie—his sister—not for me. That made it worse. If she had to borrow that much, he said, she should have skipped grad school. "I don't understand how you got in such a mess, Mom," he said. "Why did you borrow so much?" The answer—because that's what you need for grad school—made him more suspicious. This wasn't his life. Debt happened to other people, not him.

The loans poisoned my relationship with Leenie *and* Rod. I don't think of him as much as I think of Leenie but when I do it's with a jolt instead of the low throb I get with her. I should never have asked him for money. It wakes me up in the middle of the night.

More lights went on at the other end of the floor. I was still at Lenny's desk when Brian breezed through with a jacket over his shoulders. This time he pulled up a chair.

He was waiting for me to say something. I had nothing I wanted to say.

"Do you know what your problem is, Kay?"

"I can't even fake it, Brian."

"You come across...it's like you're somebody who hates innovators. Who would obstruct innovation if you could. You're like one of these people that hates Goggle. Who hates Facebook. Who hates Apple."

"So what if I think there *is* something hateful about those companies? That's not enough to get me arrested."

The puppets quaked as Brian slammed his fist on Lenny's desk. "See! I knew it!"

"Knew what?"

"It was only a matter of time before I knew it."

When he came in Brian was calm and cordial. That was over. He went from being condescending and benign to hostile and really mad.

"I think I know who you are now, Kay."

"Really?"

"You're a hater."

I looked around. "I'm a what?"

"No, you're a hater. That's the perfect category. It's handy and it would be illegal for me to hold your age against you."

"My age?"

"You're like these people who hate Google, who hate Twitter and Facebook. These haters who say the people at Apple are robber barons, who are running sweat shops in some place like China so we can have cheap cool phones. Twitter is insanely great. Google is insanely great. I love Google like I love the air we breathe. I defy anyone to say it's not great." He pounded his fist on Lenny's desk. "Google is Great! Google is Great! Google is Great!"

His voice echoed. It reminded me that no one was here. We could be having this conversation an hour from now and there would still be nobody here.

"Suppose they help put us out of business. How great will they be then, Brian?"

"No, you've got it backwards. These technologies will help us *stay* in business—*if* people like you can be proactive. To these people who say tech companies are leveraging sweat shops in some godforsaken place like China so we can get cheap cool phones, I say cool! Let the Chinese work up a sweat! Get some exercise! If they have an obesity problem in China or India or any of these other places, they won't anymore. Times are changing now the poor get fat. Why should you and I have to deal with that."

I didn't say anything.

"What do you think, Kay?"

"I'm tired. I can't think."

"Kay! You should think of something to say! And keep it short—brevity, brevity, brevity! I'd like to see your Facebook page."

"You can't."

"Why?"

"I don't have one."

Brian gasped, then smote his brow. He stood up. He sat down. "You *don't* have a Facebook page? Holy crap, Kay, that is *just insane!*"

Brian took a deep breath. "What you should do next, Kay, is get a Twitter following. Work on that."

"I hate Twitter."

"Seriously?"

"You don't have enough space to say anything of real value but just enough to say things that can be really stupid. If they gave you more space? There'd be even more stupidity. And I hate that stupid little bird."

"Are you serious?"

"People will be reductive about things that aren't simple. It will provoke them to say things that are best left unsaid and make completely asinine remarks in public. They'll say vicious things about each other and it won't matter whether or not they're true. This behavior will be everywhere. I don't wanna ride in that clown car."

Brian's voice started to rise. "That is so *wrong*, Kay. You don't understand this medium, you don't understand *life*. So you need to be on social media. This is going to be how people communicate going forward."

"It'll be how people make fools of themselves going forward. They won't be able to keep their hands off their devices, they'll be like masturbating 15-year-olds. Or masturbating 50-year-olds. And who will fact-check my twits?"

"Nobody. There's no need. This lets you put your content out fast so people can react to it. That's what makes this robust."

"What's going to happen, Brian, when people just make up shit and say it's the truth when it's not true at all?"

"So that will never happen."

"Suppose somebody says something that's true and a million people twit that it's a lie."

"It'll never happen."

"Suppose you post a lie on social media and millions of people vouch for it as fact?"

"If it happens, you just move on."

"Suppose you get more clicks for something that's totally fake, that's a complete lie, than you do for something that can be verified as true?"

"That's progress Kay. That's the soul of the new machine."

"If I'm going to post on Twitter or Facebook, Brian, I think you should pay me for it. It's extra work."

"Pardon me?"

"It could be a few bucks per message. But you're asking me to do extra work and if I'm expected to do this after I get home I'd like to be paid *something*."

"Wow. That's crazy."

"What's crazy about wanting to be paid more?"

"No, Bird Girl, that is so...*disruptive*. That is bad disruption."

"I'm not crazy for wanting to be compensated fairly."

"Kay, learn to live in the 21st Century, ok? I don't know how much you get paid, but you *are* fairly compensated."

"Not if I have to send out a bunch of messages after work along with what I already write. Messages will beget messages. I'd have to spend more time just to make sure I know what I'm talking about."

"Kay..."

"Is five dollars a twit too much?"

"That would be a finance and accounting *nightmare!*"

"It would be chump change. Management won't feel it. Pay me 25 cents per word. Two bits per word for my twits."

"Kay...that is incredibly *dumb!*"

"I never send work-related e-mail from home," I lied. "If I'm gonna be twitting, I wanna be paid."

"It's called *tweeting*, Kay."

"What if tweeting turns you into a twit?"

"Kay, you're a *tweeter* if you use *Twitter!*"

"No, you're not. You're a twit if you use Twitter."

"What do you mean by *twit?*"

"It's in the dictionary. Look it up."

"No, you started this, you define it."

"I don't want to be part of this feeding frenzy, Brian. State law says that 35 hours a week is a full-time job. I put in way more than that. Now I've got to twit when I'm off the grid? I wanna draw an X through this whole thing."

"Think about what you owe this company, Bird Girl. Think about what you owe all of us and what you *owe me.*"

"What I owe *you?*"

"That's right. You have your role here, health insurance, a 401K. You go to that goddamn gym *all the time* and it costs you practically nothing. You don't punch a clock or pay union dues. You should be grateful to add value to what we do here *any way you can.* This isn't a job, it's a role that you need to own."

Brian was getting really worked up. I tried to be calm. I imagined pushing Lenny in his wheel chair along a boardwalk in Tampa. If I hadn't met him on the sidewalk, I wouldn't know where he was going. I wanted to check e-mail to see if he wrote. But he had no way to send me an e-mail. He was probably in New Jersey by now.

Brian was solemn. "So this is really bothering you."

I looked at a spot on the wall where there used to be a clock. "Skip it. I'll be a twit if I do Twitter and I'll be a twit if I don't do Twitter."

"So do you want to share your feelings, Kay?"

"No."

"Be open. Be transparent."

"I said skip it!"

I had been trying to think of a way to get rid of him. Instead I yelled at him. I couldn't skip it anymore. He was going to want a make good for being yelled at. I tried to be subtle. I tried to think of *something.*

"Webheads talk about transparency while they stand in the shadows, Brian. My gut tells me not to trust this. That's really all I'm saying."

"Why are you thinking with your gut, Kay? Use your head, use your brain, *leverage data.*"

"You think I don't leverage data? I'm working in a data sweatshop. I'm drowning in data all day."

The blood went to Brian's face. He opened his mouth—and nothing came out. Now I'd gone too far. I'd maligned data. He looked at me and saw a data hater. I'd just outed myself. After all this time.

I felt faint. The only thing I could think about were sweat shops.

"Brian, the sweat you work up at the gym is nothing like the sweat you work up in a sweatshop, whether it's a digital one or some other kind."

"How do you know?"

"Because it isn't exercise in that sense at all. It's like stoop labor even if you're sitting down. You're physically constrained to manufacture a product. It's all fine motor skills, your aerobic system isn't engaged. You don't have to be making cool phones. You could be zipped into a hazmat suit making a prescription drug that's supposed to treat back pain but all you get are night sweats and suicidal thoughts—and your back still hurts. And the people working on assembly lines, *they* get a back problems along with hypertension and carpel tunnel syndrome."

"So how do you know so much?"

"I've read the newspaper accounts."

"Is that all? That's really weak, Kay."

"I covered the meat packing industry. Those places were worse than sweat shops. I wrote those stories, I was able to bear witness."

"For some small newspaper, no doubt."

"Bigger than the one I'm at now."

Brian looked like he was ready to explode. Then a calm settled over him. I don't know where it came from. It floated in on a cloud. It was like a spider web. The calm captured him.

"So let's change the subject," Brian said. "What are you working on?"

"What am I working on?"

"Yeah, what stories."

"Why do you want to know?"

"Why don't you want to tell?"

I looked around. "Is this a story meeting?"

"No."

"Ok. There's the multi-asset class trading story."

"Great. I've heard we can't get enough of those. What else."

"A story on Euroclear. It's about their view of settling trades in T+2, where it takes two days for sellers to get their money after the trade is executed. The industry is stuck on T+3."

"I'm not familiar with that. What else?"

"A story about the Financial Products Mark-up Language, or FpML. It's a messaging standard for the over-the-counter derivatives market based on XML, the extensible mark-up language, a self-describing meta language. There's a new version."

"What's it called?"

"FpML 5.5. They were stuck on 1.0 for years, which supported interest rate swaps and forward rate agreements. Since the 2008 crash, they've been trying to automate the entire market, which would supposedly reduce the risk that trades won't settle. They've made some headway on clearance and settlement, but the dealers still want to trade on the phone. What might help is a swap execution facility that would centralize trade execution."

"Never heard of it. What else?"

"The Bernie Madoff story."

"Which one?"

"It's about how the Madoff fraud might have been discovered by looking for FIX trader log files."

"What's that?"

"FIX is a data model that was first used to trade equities on a screen. When a trade is executed in FIX, an electronic record is created that you can trace back to the broker who submitted the trade."

"I never heard of it."

"Neither did the SEC examiners who looked at Madoff's operation. Madoff used FIX in his broker dealer business, which was legitimate, but not in his asset manager business, where the fraud was located. The story argues that if they had asked for the FIX trader log files in his fraudulent asset management business and Madoff or his underlings said, 'Sorry, no trader log files,' that would have tipped them off that something was wrong. They would have eventually discovered there were no legit records and no real trades. That would lead investigators to the fraud. Madoff was an early adopter of FIX."

A pained look crossed Brian's face. "Isn't this a negative story, Bird Girl?"

"It's fine."

"So our industry gets trashed. A *lot*, in good times and bad. Let's skip the Madoff thing and write something more positive."

"All I'm saying is that here's a potential solution that could help catch the next fraud. That's positive."

"I think you should pass on that one. We've done too much on regulation."

"Does that mean I can't do a story that compares the New York Fed's regulation of Goldman Sachs and Morgan Stanley with what the Securities and Exchange Commission did before 2008?"

"Let's do a rethink on that."

"I'm also hearing that people are on the move at FinCEN, the U.S. Treasury Department's anti-money laundering bureau. I know somebody who is naming names and saying why."

Brian brightened. "Yes! People moves rock! Every

industry loves gossip."

"And I've got one on Section 312 of the USA Patriot Act on correspondent banks. That's a big deal in anti-money laundering. There's a need to identify the beneficial owners of accounts. That can't be done now, but I've heard there's been progress."

He didn't reply and dove into his cell phone. There were wheels in the hallway. They were getting louder. The facilities guy was back with the trash barrel. Brian looked up from his phone, waited until he turned a corner. The sound faded away.

"So I'm sorry if I got huffy, Kay."

"Huffy?"

"I had a difficult night. It's not your fault."

"It's not?"

"There are just too many words chasing too few dollars. I'm new here and still trying to figure everything out and feel it out. But we're going to be cut to the bone soon. There are things we can't indulge anymore and there's nothing I can do about it. Let's go someplace where we can talk it out."

"Aren't we doing that now?"

"Let's not do it here."

"The break room?"

"How about the conference room upstairs?"

"Why there? What's wrong with here?"

"Because neither of us has a real office. There's a door we can close and shades on the window. We can have some privacy."

"Why do we need privacy?"

"Because I think David's in the building."

"Your boss? That David?"

Brian looked over his shoulder. "In fact I think he'll swing by soon. Let's not be here then."

"What's wrong with the break room?"

"It's being used. And there's no privacy. And the conference room is empty. Meet me in ten minutes?"

He left. I wondered what he was going to do that would take ten minutes. Would he get on an elevator and go up to 23? Check for David? He was dropping little hints that I couldn't read.

Privacy wouldn't be guaranteed. If David saw us in the conference room and wanted to walk in, he'd walk in.

I thought about getting paid for twitting. That would never work. I had to walk that back. Whether they paid me for my twits or my tweets—and they wouldn't pay me a plug nickel—they could also decide to pay me by the number of page views my stories got. If those numbers started to drop, so would my compensation. Somehow, I was probably going to get paid less.

I poked around Lenny's desk before I left. Things got moved after the puppets came. Lenny's desk screamed a stoic kind of chaos. It screamed *something*, even if outwardly he was calm. But he was disciplined, too. It took me a while to notice.

Everything was there except him. And there was the letter he was writing to me. I imagined him in the middle of the night trying to write this letter while I was lying awake, avoiding the numbers on the clock by my bed. What did he want to tell me that he couldn't just come right out and say?

I walked by the break room, which was a tight squeeze for four people. There were vending machines with stale candy and inedible coffee. There was one table and chairs, occupied by two snoozing cleaning ladies. If they woke up, we'd have to talk over them. And there'd be no place to sit.

I took the stairs to 23. The pizza boxes were still piled up outside the conference room. The place was empty, but the place was a mess. I walked around to the head of the table opposite the door when Brian came through it.

He sat down beside me and put his phone on the table, then his hands, like he was waiting for me to say something.

He moved closer. "So Lenny was let go."

I didn't say anything.

"It won't be official until tomorrow," he added. "It's a co-incidence that we're both here. But now that we know, I'm tipping you off about how they want you to help get a replacement."

"How am I supposed to do that?"

"There's a plan. By the way, can I ask your advice about something?"

"My advice?"

Brian seemed uncertain. "It's not about anything important."

"Is it about work?"

"It's about...something important."

"Go ahead, Brian, what is it."

"So...somebody like gave me the...opportunity to smoke some 420 at a party last night and I said no."

"This is weed, right? Not smack? Not molly or some new-fangled drug I never heard of?"

"Yup."

"And?"

"So now I'm afraid that I'm going to be perceived by these people as not being cool because I had a joint in my hand and passed on it. What should I do in that situation?"

"I don't know."

He paused. "Is that all you can say?"

"That's it."

Brian licked his lips. "So you have no advice for me? Wow. You're really hard."

Water was running in the pipes under the floor. Was this really all he wanted to talk about? Was it possible that he did four years of college without encountering some pot? I decided not ask.

"What would you like to know, Brian?"

"So how can I not do drugs and still be cool. I did drugs with people I knew in college. I thought it would end there. But it seems like I'm meeting those same people again. They're older but haven't changed. So you're experienced, you're...mature. People did drugs when you were my age. How do you negotiate this?"

"I'd say don't let somebody else define what cool is for you."

"That's a really easy answer."

"Is it?"

"So I don't know how to do that. I feel pressure to get stoned but sobriety works for me. I don't know what does and what doesn't make sense."

His phone rang. "Let me take this call."

He got up and left.

I was staring at the door, when it struck me that I never had a conversation like this with my son. Where was I when that should have happened? What was I doing? I'd had my own struggles with pot. I should have been on him about this as soon as he reached middle school. As far as I know he not only didn't experiment with drugs but had no interest.

I once smoked on the job before I decided I hated dope and nipped that habit in the bud, but not before I had been nearly caught once or twice. After you've been a pot head, hating dope can be an acquired taste. But once I decided to stop, I stopped the same day.

My kids never saw me smoke but they've seen me stoned. I wonder what would have happened if one of my editors found me in a stairwell with a joint, one toke over the line. It depended more on the editor and where I was working.

Former editors flashed before my eyes, like a slide show played on the wall of the conference room. I moved a lot with my second husband Elmer, Leenie's father. People called him El. We met in a bar in Denver after I split up with Ned, Rod's father. I was only there because a baby sitter fell into my lap that night. A whirlwind romance followed once I knew I'd struggle with single parenthood. I needed a partner and took one of the first guys that came along. I didn't know him well. My judgment wasn't good. I don't like to think about it. I was about Leenie's age.

He repaired road building equipment, mainly road graders, bulldozers and those monster dump trucks with big wheels. When he moved for work, we went with him. I left my job at the *Rocky Mountain News* and became a wandering gypsy in the newspaper business. I got as far west as Sacramento and as far east as Raleigh, North Carolina but when his business went south we ended up in his hometown. He was from Missouri, his family was there to fall back on. There was a price for that. He paid. Then I started to pay.

He'd been unemployed for a while when I took a newspaper job covering the state legislature in Jefferson City, MO, the capitol. We moved there with the kids. The second week I went to interview a state representative who was retiring. I go into his office, he closes the door and says, "Do you want to have sex with me?" Before I could take a breath he's got his hand up my skirt, like he'd done this before, like he'd had lots of practice.

I had to physically resist. I left with no interview. I didn't tell the bureau chief. Two reporters told me not to. One, a guy, covered the interview for me.

I had a different problem with Elmer. He could be insanely jealous—of everybody. If he found out about this he'd head for that esteemed state representative's office and break his face. Then I'd be going to Elmer's family for bail money. I had to keep this to myself—and from him. After a while I realized I couldn't keep this job. What bailed me out was that Elmer found work in another town. We were done with Jefferson City.

That put me out of work for a little while. By then I liked the newspaper business a lot less—and Elmer, too. I'd look at Leenie and think: maybe she needs her dad. I'd look at my finances and think: I need a job, especially if I decided to leave Elmer.

I wondered what television was like. I could have taken advantage of being over six feet tall in heels. Maybe the camera would be kind to me. But my voice is wrong. It's too low. Sometimes I slur my words. My lower teeth are funny and I never had the time or the money for braces. Once I moderated a conference panel and people complained that I was mumbling. My so-called good looks didn't help, and that's in the eye of the beholder anyway. Are you looking at my face or my body? My smile or my ass? But there's a problem every time I open my mouth and it's my voice. There was public relations, where you had to be cynical. I'm the wrong kind of cynical.

I was staring into space when the door opened. Brian was back. He walked around the table and sat next to me again. I went to get a drink from the water cooler near the door. When I came back, I sat across from him on the other side of the table and folded my hands on top.

"So Kay, what do you think about what we were discussing. About drugs."

"First, I don't do drugs."

"Not when you were young?"

"Ok, Brian, maybe I did. That was a while ago. I'd have to think about it."

The day would come when Brian would read my copy. The day could also come when somebody would edit my copy on a handheld device, their phone, where the keyboard was so small that fat-finger typos would appear that I didn't write. I could count the months, the days before I'd see that. Or years. Or never. Let the countdown begin.

Brian was tapping his phone. He looked up. "So what do you think?"

"About what?"

"I don't normally do this."

"Do what?"

"Smoke 420. I can't ask my old man about this because he can't know."

"Don't tell him."

"But if I really *did* smoke some shit, I'd feel like I'd have to tell him. So I don't dare smoke."

"I fail to see the logic."

"I can't explain this, it would take too long. Take my word for it, not telling him would be a betrayal. Telling him I smoked weed would be a betrayal, too. So he had a problem with hard drugs. That's as blunt as I'll be. It screwed up my family, his law practice and I'm afraid those genes didn't skip me. But then I think the buy-in for some social situations means getting stoned. And I can't do it because he'd hate it."

The water was running in the pipes again.

"What would your father do?" he asked.

"My father?"

"Yeah."

"About what?"

"If he found you smoking a joint."

I tried to look into Brian's eyes. Did he get stoned before he came to work? Did he do more than smoke dope? Was that how he got through the day?

"Brian, I've gone as far as I'm gonna go with this."

"With what?"

"With *this*. I've listened to your problem and given you an opinion, but we leave my father out of it. I don't owe you a discussion about that and a lot of other things."

Brian took a deep breath. He took it slow. He made an odd sound when he exhaled. "You're really hard, aren't you Kay?"

There was a pause. It got longer. I didn't know what it meant.

Brian licked his lips. "I like that. I like that a lot. Your hardness, I mean."

The pause began again.

"So is all this hardness work-related, Kay? Or is it related to something else?"

I stood up. The idea that I had no place to go but my desk was innervating. I was lucky I had that.

"Brian, it *is* a little early in the morning for this. I gotta go."

He reached across the table and grabbed my right arm, then my other arm and pulled. Before I knew it, he had me face down on the table. We were struggling. He wouldn't let go and was pulling my head toward his crotch. I flipped over, I don't know how, and broke free of his grip. My hair was in my face. I couldn't see.

He was breathing hard. "Well, even though it's early, you look fetching in that sweater, Kay."

"What?"

"And your hardness? That makes *me* hard."

"What?"

"I hope you're not going to tell me you're wearing a pullover."

"It's a pullover."

"It's a sweater. I'd love to take it off, just pull it over your head so your arms got tangled up in it and you'd struggle. I'd like to push your face—"

I picked up a mug and threw coffee at him. I missed. "Brian! You asshole! You can't scorn me one minute, ask me for advice the next, make remarks about my appearance and then..."

"And then what?"

"And then act like a complete asshole! What the fuck do you think this is!"

Brian's face fell. Suddenly he seemed crestfallen. He was fumbling for words. "You mean you...you're not ...this doesn't make you hot?"

"Brian! Stop it! Right now!"

"But, Kay, I'm a younger guy, you're an older woman. Doesn't this make you feel...flattered?"

"No! I am not flattered! I'll break your fucking jaw!"

His face turned red. His jaw stuck out, like he wouldn't be able to pull it back into his head. For several moments I thought he was going to explode. The moments kept coming.

Then he held up his hand like a traffic cop. His tone of voice changed. "Ok. So there's something they're going to ask you to do."

"Wait. What did you just do to me?"

"David and his group. They want you to go chat up the editor at *Pension Benefit Wire*."

"What did you just say to me?"

"Go over to 99 Wall Street, the 20th floor. Chat him up. Tell him what it's like to work here."

"Really?"

"Absolutely."

"Brian—what's it like to work here?"

"So this is serious, Kay. You can make a good impression. We've got to get somebody to replace Lenny and you know them, right?"

"I don't know them."

"You told me you did."

"I *never* told you that."

"It doesn't matter. Go there, look for Devon, chat him up."

"Who?"

"He's the guy you're going to meet at *Pension Benefit Wire*. That's a worse dump than here, he'll be grateful to move to our digs. David wants him and we need you to make the introduction." His phone buzzed. "Wait—I gotta take this."

Brian left, tripping over a chair as he went.

The door was left open. He came back and closed it.

I looked at one arm, then the other. They looked the same. Tomorrow there might be a bruise on one. Or both.

I was thinking about airplanes taking off and landing at a faraway airport. I wasn't on any of them. The west coast was three hours behind the east coast. Rod was still asleep with his wife. I didn't normally think of my son when I needed a distraction. I was thinking of him now.

I imagined him walking to work, entering his office, sitting at his desk. A young woman walked up to him, asked a question. He answered, and she walked away. Would he ever behave like Brian? I have a feeling he never would. I'm sure he wouldn't but I have a feeling that I also don't know him well. More than a feeling.

While I had that feeling, sepia-toned images danced around in a faraway photo album. There was Rod sleeping in his crib as a six-month-old. Rod falling down as he learned to walk. Rod on his tricycle. Rod petting our pussy cat. Suddenly I wanted to hold him in my arms, as an infant. I wanted to smell that baby smell once more, even if it was really talcum powder.

I could remember the smell of our house in Denver. I imagined that Ned and I stayed together in that house and I never married Elmer, never went to bed with him, never even met him or found a babysitter that night. I imagined that Ned didn't have a breakdown. I imagined that he tried to be a better parent and that we were happy. Not a default kind of happiness—but *really happy!* But what about Leenie? If I never met Elmer, there'd be no Leenie. There could be another kid with Ned, but it wouldn't be her.

Brian ducked his head in. His voice was creaky. "Kay?"

"Brian, we gotta talk."

"Not now. We have to focus on Devon."

I slammed my fist on the table. "Brian! Goddamit you fucking assaulted me!"

"Kay, I don't know what you're getting so excited about. We need to grab Devon now. He doesn't have a non-compete agreement. After you see him, we'll go talk to David."

I was stuttering.

"Kay, I can't discuss the other stuff, the stuff you and I did just did now. But maybe later."

I couldn't speak.

"Just go. He knows you're coming. In fact, I'd say go now."

Brian left. I was alone in the conference room like I was on Saturday night.

In a few hours, the handful of people that were left would trickle in. They'd hear the news about Lenny and think, *ok, so there's no Lenny. Is there still a paper? Do I still work here?* Nobody left was important enough to get face time with anyone above Brian. After an e-mail or two, he might come by the newsroom, what was left of it, for a chat.

The good thing about Brian was that he worked on a different floor. This was going to give me time to think, especially if this newspaper was falling apart at the seams.

Or at the staples. I imagined the paper turning yellow around the staples. I imagined the inserts falling all over the floor. Right now there was no editor. And it never had staples.

Chapter Seven

I grabbed my handbag and went to the lobby. Instead of going to *Pension Benefit Wire,* I stopped near the entrance. On Monday a guy with a hand truck dropped 100 copies of *SIN* in the lobby. People opened the plastic wrap and grabbed some before the rest went upstairs.

I didn't know what to do about Brian. This wasn't over. Something was just starting even if I couldn't be sure what it was and I didn't see it coming. In one hour, he went from someone I didn't think about to this guy who grabbed me when we were alone in the conference room, propositioned me, assaulted me, then asked me to poach somebody from another trade paper and bring him back like a trophy—if that's what just happened. Was I really going to sit through a meeting with Brian and David like nothing happened?

This was happening too fast. Things slowed down just enough for me to understand I was probably fucked or about to be. It was a question of how and when.

Maybe this was a one-time thing. Or this could happen again. If I complained Brian would retaliate. If I didn't complain he might think he could get away with this. What just happened could be a prelude to the next incident.

I had to stop this before it got out of hand. This stopped me in my tracks. I had to come up with a response. That's what I was waiting for, not the next issue of *SIN.*

I tried to outline a complaint in my head. But I would be fucked there, too. The complaint would go to the HR director. She and Brian were buddies. I'd known her for years and we didn't get along. I'd have nobody on my side.

I started outlining a complaint again. The argument we had kept getting in the way. Did he really call me *Bird Girl* before we went to the conference room? That pissed me off almost as much as anything and I could actually get him to stop calling me Bird Girl, even apologize.

There was probably nothing I could do about the rest. He could say that he was paying me an innocent complement about my looks and it got out of hand. And I called him an asshole. But he grabbed my arms and yanked me across the table and I noticed that my wrist hurt. And he tried to yank off my pullover. Did he really do that? If this was the first time anyone called him out on something like this and he promised not to do it again, is he off the hook?

We were alone in the conference room. It would be my word against his. Maybe I could trade on the fact that I'd been here much longer than he had. Suppose I took him aside first, had a talk and straightened him out. Suppose that led to total war.

This happened to me once before at another job. I wanted to slam the door on this whole thing for a while and come back to it later. If I complained, management could make it all go away by getting rid of me in the next round of lay-offs. They'd say it was the budget. They wouldn't even say that. They'd just can me.

I couldn't deal with it now. I was thinking of faraway places. I had no place to go but 99 Wall Street.

I never wanted to come here. I often forget that. Leenie, Rod and I came to New York from Missouri after

I left Leenie's father. I had to get out of the town we lived in and away from his family—and him. I thought about Nashville but that wasn't far enough. I thought New York would be a place where Elmer wouldn't be caught dead—and I was right, although I was looking over my shoulder for a long time. I had no job contacts. I knew no one.

We got lucky with the apartment but had no furniture, we were sleeping on the floor. The kids had sleeping bags. Leenie was bullied by a grade school posse. We didn't always have food. I can remember being hungry. I remember feeling faint.

That's when I came to this company. I had interviews with three separate publications. None of them wanted me. I would have taken anything besides a reporter job. I would have washed windows or picked up the trash.

Somehow Lenny found me. He had an opening at *SIN* that wasn't advertised—back then they put ads in newspapers. We talked. We went out for tea and talked some more. He sat me down with a diagram that described straight-through processing, or STP, and how transactions in the securities industry were moving from paper records to computers. Follow this diagram, he said, and it will unlock this job.

I'd never reported on tech or finance before. When he hired me I was $25 short of covering the next month's rent. I got paid on the 31st of that month. The check cleared on the 1st. I wanted to thank him. I didn't. I couldn't let on that I was that close to the edge.

Every day I came to work thinking it would be my last, afraid of what Lenny was going to say. After I had been there a while and was learning the beat, he started to soften. He went from somebody I hated to see to somebody I looked forward to seeing. Not many people like their boss. Whether I liked him or not, I thought I owed him for taking a chance on me. He wanted nothing in return. Maybe I didn't owe him after all.

Pretty soon I'm working six days a week. That wasn't soft. I was in fief to the Global Straight-Through Processing Association, which was supposed to facilitate cross-border trade matching between investment managers and broker dealers. I boned up on the Basel II Accords, which had to do with the amount of cash reserves banks had to maintain. The FATF 40 Recommendations and Title III of the USA Patriot Act, which was supposed to prevent financial crime, kept me up at night. So did MiFID, the Markets in Financial Instruments Directive, part of a European Union regulatory regime I don't completely understand. Trillions of dollars—and trillions of euros—were at stake. Still, I saw a trade press prol when I looked in the mirror every morning.

For me to survive, all this had to become absolutely fascinating, the most interesting thing in the world. That was a lot of work. But it started to make sense, the concepts you have to know seemed less abstract and Lenny was starting to trust me. The kids started doing well in public school. My feet were on the ground at last.

I was thinking that I'd work here for a few years until something better came along. Nothing came along. This place is what came along. The reporter that sat closest to me, Kara Markakis, was about my age, lived in Staten Island with her parents and had been here longer than Lenny. She worked seven days a week because she didn't know what else to do with herself. She was unable to speak in a conversational tone of voice. She yelled. I'd heard that it wasn't the job that made her like that. She came here that way.

Thanksgiving and Christmas were her two worst days of the year because no one was allowed in the building. Management exploited her as she did the work of two people. Kara and two other reporters, Mary Melvin and Beverly Levine, both SIN lifers, both single and middle-aged, were the only ones left besides me.

We weren't exactly friends. When we talked, we talked shop. I don't know how they'd react to a story about Brian.

I couldn't tell Kara about this. She would tell the world, intimating that I brought this on myself, then deny she'd told anyone. Mary and Bev were beyond jaded. They might have their own Brian stories. If I told Mary she'd swear at Brian, ask if I was ok but leave it there. Beverly Levine would peek over her horn-rimmed glasses and say, "So Brian hit on you. So what? I want outa here!" Finding another job and leaving *SIN* was her grim preoccupation. She'd been looking for years. There wasn't another job for her.

Every Monday morning when the paper arrived, she carefully cut out her stories and added them to her *SIN* clip file. She had photocopied versions, PDFs and laminated copies suitable for framing. *SIN* didn't have an online archive that went beyond six months. Older stories disappeared.

I avoided this to a fault. My own clip file was in disarray. Sometimes I saved my stories and sometimes I didn't. In the bargain I lost track of dozens that were flawed on one hand but really good on the other.

One night on the A train I looked down to avoid the gaze of a stranger and saw an issue of *SIN* on the floor. It didn't come into focus right away. It was opened from the inside and flipped over so you could see the front and the back page. *SIN* never went beyond certain offices or industry conferences. You wouldn't find it left on the subway.

There was a story on the front page with my byline, smeared with footprints, like it had been on the floor of the A train since Brooklyn. Before I knew it, somebody was standing on it. I couldn't pick it up. I wanted to ask the guy to move but hesitated. The story was about the future of foreign exchange trading— would it be phone based or screen based? It would obviously be screen based, but you could trade any way you wanted if you were wealthy enough.

I got into an argument with Lenny over how to write this. I got my way, but he was miffed and I never saw it in print. A month later I was trying to read that story on the floor of a subway car with somebody standing on it.

As though it had legs, the paper moved across the floor next to somebody else's feet. Then another guy walked on top of it. "Excuse me," I said, "but you're standing on my story. You have no idea how hard I worked on this and I don't have a copy."

He backed away. The paper was torn. I was going to leave it on the floor. It might as well have been a donut wrapper. I picked it up and took it home. My only copy was in tatters. It wasn't worth saving. I saved it.

I wouldn't have reacted that way if it was a web page that crashed. It's not just because of the way an idiotic Twitter message, a devious Facebook post and a well-written newspaper article are all defined as *content* in the digital scheme of things. Something different happens in my brain when I read words on a screen than when I read them on paper. I concentrate differently with paper, part of my mind closes down when I'm on a screen. I can't explain it but it's visceral,

I can feel it. Maybe this will change.

It reminds me of the difference between running on a treadmill and running on solid ground. It's still running, but the treadmill, is different. The surface underneath your feet is moving the way the words on a screen are back lit and sometimes shimmer. Words on paper aren't like words etched in stone but they have permanence. Once they're printed on paper, you can't change them, you can't take them back. You're stuck with them. It's like painting. When paint goes on a canvas, something changes. You can't change it back.

Chapter Eight

I stayed in the lobby a little longer. It was light out but there was no newspaper. I took a few steps out the door, then stopped. If Len called, I wouldn't be at my desk and couldn't answer. He could stop the car, pull over and find a phone booth. It wasn't impossible. All I wanted was to hear that he was ok.

I started to get teary. This was my dear friend. I don't think he understood that. I was hurt that he couldn't tell me he was leaving and I had to find out by accident. It made me want to rent my own car and skip town. I'd stalk Lenny all over Tampa until I found him. What I would do then I didn't know.

The Alzheimer's diagnosis was probably real the way *SIN* would close inside of a year. He probably didn't want to tell me what he knew. If the end was near, I'd find out soon enough. Hearing it from him would have made me feel a little better and make him feel a little worse. I should have known.

I needed some cash. I could have waited until after *Pension Benefit Wire* but I walked by a bank. The main lobby was closed but the cash machine annex was open. There was nobody there. I got out my debit card. I began to dip it, then stopped.

I remembered the letter on Lenny's desk. The collection agency letter, not the one he was writing me. Was the loan in default? Was my bank account frozen?

The numbers on the calculator were dim but I could read them. It had been a year since I started making payments on the PLUS Loans. The first three payments were made to the servicer in Missouri—then the loan was switched to Fedloan. The next nine payments went by mistake to the Stafford Loan, not the PLUS Loan I co-signed, which hadn't been paid for nine months.

Each month had thirty days for accounting purposes. Nine times 30 equaled 270 days. That was the magic number that put you in default—and there had been no payment to the PLUS loan for 270 days at least. I didn't know if my math was wrong. I keyed in more numbers. I was feeling faint.

I was afraid to dip my card because of what would be on the screen. If I didn't fix this, I could lose control of my bank account. I was afraid it was already too late. This happened to my second husband's brother, who owed money on a pickup truck. First they took his truck, then a collection agency came after his money. His bank account was constantly being frozen. Elmer, Leenie's father, was smug because nothing like that happened to us. All these years later it was happening to me. I thought of the money I made when Ned and I sold the house in Denver all those years ago. Where did it go?

I had no idea what would happen next. Having collection agency fees on top of a garnishment could bring me to a different place. It could be less bad than I thought. If *SIN* closed after this started and I was on the street, it could ruin me. The idea plucked me off a sidewalk in New York and dropped me in some wilderness. I could ask Rod for money again. I was thinking, again, that Leenie was the favorite, Rod was second fiddle. A lot of good that did her.

I was physically afraid of Leenie's father by the time we left. He'd hidden loaded guns all over our house, which belonged to his parents. He adored Leenie, he said, but by then hated me. I found out that he had threatened to kill somebody who hit on me at the local hardware store.

I didn't tell Leenie about that. Instead I told her that her father didn't love me anymore and that's why we had to go. We left on a Wednesday afternoon while he was at work. If he'd caught us leaving, I think he would have shot me.

I tried to answer all of her other questions. "If he doesn't love you," she said, "do you still love him? When did you know he didn't love you anymore? What is love?" Explain that to a five-year-old. Or a thirty-five-year-old.

Convincing her that we had to leave was the hardest thing I've ever done. Rod was easier to convince. It was Leenie's father, not his. Leenie was never convinced. I made her leave her father when she was a little girl. I never told her the whole story.

The thing that shocked me was the way he just let us go. Leenie never really forgave me. But the way her father faded away made it easier. I expected him to fight me, demand to see her, stalk me for the rest of my life and he didn't. He stayed away. For years I searched local Missouri papers for with this name. Nothing turned up.

Leenie was going to have to *do something*—as in *earn more money*. I worried again that she was becoming someone who would never earn much. I was pacing around, rehearsing the speech I'd make if she were here, writing it down on deposit slips. She was young, I hoped there was still time for her. If she had to be a better woman than I am, great—I'd be proud of her. She couldn't let my mistakes define her. She had to rise above that. She could do it. I know she could.

A man came in and I threw the speech in a trash can. Leenie went to grad school to have adult experiences. She needed loans to get there. This is how people live now, right? Getting a job was supposed to be her adult experience. Instead it was getting a loan.

And now it was really on me. Depending on what happens next, it could be *me* having my Social Security benefits garnished, not her. I never thought it would be me. I'd picked up the idea she was going to be screwed because I was her mother. I never once thought that it was *me* who might get screwed because *she* was my daughter.

I waited a long time before I dipped the debit card. The collection agency letter was in my head but my account was still open. No money had been taken out. I withdrew $40. If I gave $10 to Grace Fong, it was really $30. As I was leaving I remembered Esther Kluger, who lived across the hall before Grace and Wensi. I think I borrowed $5 from Esther. I never paid her back. Esther was dead. I could feel the money changing hands.

On the way to *Pension Benefit Wire* I stopped in the office. The sun was lighting up the lobby, even though the day was going to be overcast. But it was still empty. The floor was being waxed by a facilities guy with a machine that was like a lawn mower with no wheels. The paper hadn't come. It wasn't 9:00 yet. When I got on the elevator, I was alone.

I got off on 22. There was no sign of Brian. I stopped by my desk for lip balm. I opened a drawer and noticed Lenny's desk. The top was completely bare.

There was nothing there. No computer and none of his stuff. The desk was wiped clean. No picture of Chloe, no puppets, no piles of paper. No Babe Ruth, no Jonathan Winters.

I was riffling his drawers like they were in my

bedroom. All I saw was the bottom. There was nothing to rifle.

A facilities guy came by. It was Miles Hoyt, who got hired when I did. Miles was from Mobile, Alabama and talked about going back there. He once said to me, "You never gonna retire from this place. The longer you work here, the less chance you got of stayin here that long."

At first, I didn't think that made any sense. As time went by and I watched people leave, it did.

He was straightening the cornrows down the side of his head as he came over to see what I was doing.

"What up. Y'all lookin for somethin?"

"Miles, what happened to Lenny's stuff? The box is still here but everything else is gone…"

Miles looked in one of the drawers, then at his desk. "Yeah, you know you right. Stuff is gone. The box still here."

"What happened?"

He shrugged. "I don't make them decisions. I fill some boxes only sometimes."

"How come you didn't fill his box?"

"That ain't on me." He turned and walked away.

"Where are you going?"

He gave me this little nod. "Do I know where I'm going? No, I don't. But I know where I'm coming from."

He left.

I took the elevator to the basement where they put the trash. There was a basement and some sub-basements. I went to the bottom. I wanted some of the stuff that was on Lenny's desk. I wanted to save anything I could find. I didn't know what I was going to do with it if I found it. Every time somebody left their space remained empty, sometimes for months. Then you couldn't remember who sat there, depending on who it was.

The ceilings were high and there was a large, silver garage door that trucks backed through. The walls were gray and there was an echo. The slightest sound had a ping on the end. There were rows of metal trash bins, a little like dumpsters. They were just low enough so that I didn't need a step ladder.

I found something to stand on and climbed in one. I went from bin to bin, climbing in one, climbing out, climbing into another. I was standing on mounds of paper and plastic waste. Desktop computers and screens, keyboards and mice, printers and cables. Old ink cartridges were like banana peels I could slip on. Paper, paper, everywhere, but not on Lenny's desk. People who looked at those puppets every day would walk by and notice. Sooner or later someone would say, "What happened to that old guy with the puppets?"

My eye went to something that glinted. The glass eye of one of the puppets was wedged in between a computer monitor and a trash bag in a corner of a bin. I had to climb over boxes of paper to reach it. As I pulled it out, I tore a hole in the puppet's dress. I was standing on this pile of computer waste, clutching the puppet as I climbed out. If Lenny could pick one thing, what would he want to save? The photo of Chloe or one of the puppets? I imagined him in a rented car, just outside Atlantic City. It was October. The Jersey shore traffic would be light. I thought if he made it as far as the Carolinas, he wouldn't turn back.

I put the puppet on the top of a fire hose that hung from the wall. The most recent junk would probably be in the bin where I found the puppet. I climbed back in.

I started to move things from the left side of the bin to the right. I stopped when I saw how much there was. I started half-heartedly picking things up and tossing them around. I couldn't spend all day on this. I could only carry so much stuff.

The big silver door I was gazing at started to open.

A truck was on the other side. After the door went up, it backed in toward the bins. I climbed out and watched. It was like the garbage trucks that go down my street. A couple of guys got out. This mechanism picked up the steel bins I had been climbing around in and dumped them into the back of the truck like they were toys. After they had done a few I took the puppet and left.

I rode the elevator to the lobby. I was about six blocks from 99 Wall Street. I decided to take the puppet with me to *Pension Benefit Wire*. I could put my hand inside the puppet head and provide a running commentary from Lenny. It would break the ice. If only I were a ventriloquist. I'd put on a show. It would be macabre. The guy from *Pension Benefit Wire* would never want to work for *SIN*.

It started to rain. I had my hand inside the puppet and it was like wearing a glove. I could feel how flimsy it was, how fragile and old. I stopped beside a building where the roof hung over the sidewalk, just enough so that I wouldn't get wet.

I noticed Miles walking down the other side of the street. What was he doing here? If he was on break, it must be 10:45. That means I'd been in the sub-basement for almost two hours. It was really late. There was no one there when I left. There might be no one there when I got back.

Somebody passing by glanced at the puppet. Then somebody else looked at it and looked at me. When I went by a trash can I threw the puppet in. A block later I had a crazy notion that Lenny would walk by, look in the trash can and find it. I stopped and turned around. He wasn't there.

I was so tired. The trick would be trying to stay awake. Around 1 or 2 in the afternoon, I'd fall asleep at my desk. When I dropped off, Lenny wouldn't be there to say, "Kay! You're snoring!"

Born in Camden, New Jersey, John Sandman has been a journalist for over three decades. His work has appeared in numerous publications, from the jazz magazine *Down Beat* to *The Journal of the International Association of Physicians in AIDS Care* to *US News & World Report* and a start-up at the *Financial Times* covering the property & casualty insurance industry. At *TheStreet.com*, he covered student debt with a focus on loan servicers, for-profit colleges and the U.S. Department of Education. He wrote about high-end real estate for *The Wall Street Journal.*.

He received a 2013 award from the Society of Silurians, a New York City newspaper group, for a story about internet payday lending that appeared in *City Limits*. He was part of a team of reporters that won a Jesse H. Neal award for reporting on the 2001 attack on the World Trade Center for *Securities Industry News*, then owned by what is now Thomson Reuters.

His first novel was published in Toronto by House of Anansi Press. He's received numerous writing grants from the Canada Council, the Ontario Arts Council and the Ludwig Vogelstein Foundation.

www.ingramcontent.com/pod-product-compliance
Lightning Source LLC
Chambersburg PA
CBHW070558130626
46556CB00001B/207